Gentlemen Pre

Samantha

CW00521382

Prologue

Lulworth, Dorset 1817

"I always thought you far too logical to believe in curses." Arabella leaned over to snatch up a slice of shortbread, popped it into her mouth, then declared, "I am giving up all things sweet, I swear. They are going straight to my hips."

Merry shook her head with a smile. Arabella had been saying that for the past decade, since she realized she had hips. The curvy figure of her friend had them all quite envious and Merry recalled the time they had all stuffed themselves for at least a week to try to emulate Arabella's hips and breasts. Merry had finally grown into her body only a few years ago but she never garnered any attention from menfolk—unlike Arabella.

"Why have I never heard of this curse?" Sophia asked, drifting over from the bookcase and coming to sit on the chaise longue opposite Merry.

Merry eyed her two friends. Sophia was the opposite of Arabella, despite being her older sister. Short and delicate, her dark hair contrasted with Arabella's honey tones and her features were stronger.

"Because it is nonsense," Merry answered, lifting her chin.

Sophia frowned at her. "And yet, you still fear for Daniel's marriage?"

Merry sighed. It sounded ridiculous. Even she questioned herself whenever the thought popped into her mind—what if all the terrible marriages in her family were due to the family curse?

"I just wish to give Daniel and Isabel a little space."

Arabella shook her head. "By moving into the old dower house?" She wrinkled her nose. "No one has set foot in it for a good twenty years."

"I know." Merry traced the lace edging of her sleeve with one finger. "If not longer. But I cannot stay here while my brother and his new wife try to adjust to married life. Father is never around, and it shall just be me." She looked up at her friends. "Can you imagine it? Me sitting at the large dining table whilst they are looking lovingly at each other? I should rather take up residence in the dower house than be the awkward relative no one wants around."

"I very much doubt your brother would not want you around," Sophia said. "He loves you dearly. Besides, what does your father have to say about you moving into the dower house? He cannot like the idea, surely?"

Merry shrugged. "He does not care either way. You know what he is like."

Her friends nodded sadly.

"What is this so-called curse anyway?" demanded Sophia.

Merry grimaced. She didn't believe in curses, really she did not. But the story of the family curse had plagued their family for hundreds of years. She drew in a breath. "Apparently in the 16th Century, one of my ancestors seduced a gypsy. When he left her to marry a noblewoman, the gypsy cursed him and his family."

"And?" Sophia pressed, a piece of shortbread lifted to her mouth.

"Our family and all our ancestors would never have a happy marriage," Merry said simply.

"Goodness." Sophia took a bite of shortbread and spoke through the mouthful. "So there was no way of lifting the curse?"

Merry sent her a look. "There is no curse."

Sophie leaned forward. "But if there were, is there any way of lifting it?"

Shaking her head, Merry lifted the teapot and poured another cup of tea, dropping in two sugars and adding a dash of milk. All the while she could feel Sophia's gaze on her. She met her friend's eager gaze. "There is really no curse, Sophia."

"So why do you feel the need to give Daniel and Isabel the best chance?" Arabella asked, folding her arms across her chest.

"It's only fair." Merry took a sip of tea and savored the sweet warmth. She should have never mentioned the curse. It was ridiculous. Curses were not real and even if they were, it was only a silly story, probably made up hundreds of years ago and passed down by each generation since. "But, you must admit, our family does not have a reputation for making the best matches."

"So the curse is real," Sophia said, awe tinging her voice.

"Of course it isn't," Merry snapped. "Unfortunately, us Bradfords just seem to make terrible husbands and wives. Remember my Aunt May. She got..." Merry lowered her voice and glanced around, "divorced."

Sophia put a hand to her mouth. "Goodness. And everyone else's marriages?"

"There isn't a single happy one between them. My cousin Geoffrey does not even see his wife. He spends his time in Scotland while she lives in Europe for the most part. And my cousins' parents are no better." She lifted her hands. "For some reason, we are all terrible at marriage."

"Well, I am certain Daniel will be different," Sophia declared. "He's a fine man and will treat Isabel beautifully."

Merry could not disagree there. It had been clear since his engagement to her that he adored her endlessly and they made a wonderful couple. However, that niggling thought would not leave her. She could not bear it if her brother ended up miserable in his marriage.

So, it was best she move out of the main house and into the dower house that had not been used since her great-grandma's time. She had yet to even step foot in the place, so goodness knows what state it was in.

"Anyway, once Daniel sends word he is on his way home from his honeymoon, I shall make preparations to move into the house." Merry glanced at the bookcase behind Sophia. She didn't think there would be too much to do, just a little dusting and moving around of furniture, but she would need to take her books.

"Will you not get lonely, Merry?" Arabella took another slice of shortbread, eyeing it with annoyance before taking a bite.

"Why would I? Are you all going to abandon me as soon as I move in?" Merry teased.

"It does seem like a bit of a spinster aunt thing to do," Sophia said cautiously.

"Well, I am not yet an aunt, but truthfully, I am looking forward to the solitude. I can work on my translation in peace then." Merry gave her friends a reassuring smile.

In many ways, Daniel marrying had given her the perfect excuse to leave the big house. Even though most of the time it was just her and Daniel, the house was a constant bustle of people. If tenants were not visiting, then servants were sweeping through or friends were visiting her brother. She needed complete solitude to concentrate on her translation, and the dower house would provide that.

"People are going to think you are awfully strange," Arabella cautioned.

"Do people not already think I am strange? Do they not think that of all of us?" Merry asked.

Sophia nodded, and Arabella gave a defeated shrug. Since their younger years, they had all been known as wallflowers. Their friendship group had formed out of necessity when it had become apparent that all of them were terrible at the things which young ladies should be excellent—none of them were particularly refined or accomplished in the traditional manner, and they all loathed balls and polite conversation.

Merry was no stranger to gossip, having overheard many a conversation about what a shame it was that the daughter of the viscount was not prettier or more sociable or more inclined to dancing with eligible gentleman. Her propensity for tucking herself away with books had never been looked upon favorably by others.

"I—"

The door to the drawing room burst open. A flurry of skirts and red hair paused in front of them. The footman barreled in after her, looking disconcerted. "Uh, Miss Arabella Ryder to see you, my lady."

"Thank you, Hughes." Merry dismissed the footman and eyed her friend who was currently bent double, sucking in breaths of air.

Though she shared the same name as Arabella, this Arabella could not be more different. While the seated Arabella tended to act with caution, Merry doubted this Arabella had ever acted with caution in her entire life. When they had all first met, she and Sophia used to tease the Arabellas, calling them one and two but had tired of that quickly, so now Arabella Two was known as Bella.

Bella sucked in a breath. "Have you heard the news?" She straightened. "Goodness, I sprinted all the way here and nearly knocked into Mr. Gainsborough and tripped over a sheep."

Sophia giggled. "Poor sheep."

Bella shot her a glare. "Poor *me,* I nearly died trying to jump over him."

"Sit down, Bella," Arabella ordered. "You look as though you are going to pass out any moment."

Bella pressed a hand to her stomach and drew in another long breath. "Have you heard the news?"

Merry glanced at her friend's blank faces and shook her head. "What news?"

"Miss Lucy Gable...oh poor Lucy...was *discovered*." Bella hissed the last word.

"Discovered how?" Sophia asked.

"With a man." Bella finally slumped down on the chaise next to Sophia. "Completely and utterly ruined. Her family sent her away to Ireland. We shall never see her again."

Merry winced and swung a look at Arabella. Her cheeks had already paled and Merry noticed the cup shook slightly in her hand. If anyone understood ruination, it was Arabella. A few years ago, she had been promised marriage by an eligible man, but he had run off to America after taking her innocence. Fortunately for Arabella, few people knew what had happened, so she never had to hide in Ireland, but Merry knew Arabella still nursed heartbreak over it, and Merry suspected she had always secretly hoped the man would return for her one day.

"Poor Lucy," murmured Arabella.

Silence fell over the room as they contemplated their friend's fate. Merry had known Lucy since they were little girls. She had come from a respectable family and Lucy was sweet and funny. Had she remained untouched, she would have likely married well. Merry curled her fists. How dare one man ruin it all for her? It was so unfair. She peered at each of her friends and she had no doubt they were thinking similarly.

"What is it with these men?" The words tumbled from Merry's mouth.

Their heads snapped up, mouths dropping open at her sudden declaration.

"You know what I mean." Merry stood. "Your late husband was an absolute beast," she said to Sophia who shrugged and nodded. "You were treated abominably, Arabella." She turned to Bella. "And we all know your brothers and father are vile to you. Not one of us has had a good experience with men."

"I cannot deny that," Sophia agreed.

Merry huffed. "I would quite happily never set eyes on another man and I swear I shall never marry. Never, ever."

"Hear, hear." Bella lifted her cup and giggled.

"I say we make a vow," Merry declared.

Arabella lifted a brow. "A vow?"

"Yes, a vow. We swear to remain spinsters for all our lives. Instead of worrying about men, we shall occupy ourselves with our hobbies, our friends, and our families." She paused and glanced at Bella. "That is, if we wish," she added. Bella's five brothers tormented her to no end and were notoriously awful people. No doubt she would not wish to devote any more time to them than she had to. Sophia had married young to escape them, but her marriage had been no better.

"I have no desire to marry again anyway. One arranged match is enough for me, and I can look after myself now that I am independently wealthy." Sophia stood. "I'm willing to take that vow." She looked at Arabella. "And you know I can look after you too. You need never marry."

"I shall inherit a small sum one day," Merry confirmed. "I have no need of a husband if I live frugally." They all looked to Bella.

She swung her gaze between them then stood. "Well, I am not so sure how I shall look after myself, but I'll figure it out."

"It's a deal then." Merry put out her hand. "We will remain spinsters, no matter what life puts in our way. Should any of us ever be tempted by men, we vow to protect each other."

Everyone nodded and thrust out their hands. Bella paused and drew back her hand. "We should make a blood oath."

Arabella scowled. "A blood oath? I am certainly not slicing open my hand."

"Very well, we shall spit on our hands then. Seal the deal like men." Bella spat on her hand and thrust it out.

With a shrug, Sophia did the same. Merry rolled her eyes and followed suit, eyeing Arabella. "Well?"

"Oh, very well then." Arabella spat on her hand and thrust it into the middle. They placed their hands one on top of the other. Arabella made a sound of disgust.

Merry wrinkled her nose and tried to ignore the rather wet sensation. "We do solemnly vow to remain spinsters, and to protect one another from anything or anyone who might cause us physical or emotional harm. We shall ignore the opposite sex and devote our time to our own passions and sisterhood." She looked around at her friends. "Will that do?"

"Yes." Arabella tugged her hand away and pulled a handkerchief out of her sleeve to wipe her hand. "If you ever tell anyone we did that, I shall disown you all as friends."

Bella chuckled and sat. "You wouldn't dare. You love us too much."

"Perhaps," Arabella conceded, lowering herself onto the chair.

"Arabella has a point though. We must keep these vows a secret. No one can know of our Spinster Club," Merry ordered.

"Is that what we are now? A spinster club?" Sophia asked.

"Yes." Merry gave a decisive nod. "We are the Spinster Club. And we do not talk about the Spinster Club to anyone, do we all understand?"

Chapter One

Smiling to himself, Harcourt took long strides up toward the large expanse of grassland that surrounded Whitely Grange. Trees dotted the land at random intervals, but he was only interested in one tree.

Or to be more precise, one woman who happened to be sitting underneath said tree. She did not notice him approach even though he made no secret of striding up the slope to join her. Merry's head was dipped low, a book clasped in her hands, her knees drawn up to act as a book rest. He had no doubt there would be furrows between her brows as she studied the words with precision. He'd never met a woman who could get so lost in books.

He came to a stop only a few feet from her. Sure enough, there were the furrows. He grinned to himself. Her lips were pursed, and she chewed on the end of her thumb. He could not make out the title of the book but no doubt it was some Greek myth or tragedy. If he did not know better, he'd have assumed Merry was born with a book in hand. Her obsession with Greek myths had given him plenty to tease her over these past years.

When she did not lift her head, he moved himself deliberately, sidestepping until his body blocked the sun and cast a shadow across her book. She ignored him, her focus entirely on the book. He studied her boldly, hands clasped behind his back.

At around eighteen, Merry had grown into a fully-fledged woman. He still recalled her birthday and the strange awakening it created in him. Merry was no longer his closest friend's sister. She was a woman. The realization had sent him reeling. He'd grown a little more accustomed to it now and at the age of twenty, so had she. Gone were the awkward braids that made her look like a child, and she dressed with a subtle feminine flair that he doubted was deliberate. With her inky black hair twisted up, delicate curls escaped and touched her neck. When she unpinned it, it would be a riot of curls—something she complained about frequently. His fingers twitched. What would she do if he just leaned in and plucked those pins away to send it spilling all over?

Shoot him a look that would kill probably.

He coughed and rocked on his heels. Merry flicked a page and he saw her gaze whisk over the words. He pressed his lips together. She must have seen him by now. Even she could not be that absorbed in a book. The minx was simply playing with him. He coughed again.

Her gaze remained on the book. "That's a terrible cough you have there, Harry. I think you should see a doctor."

"I could probably drop dead right here, and you would not notice."

She lifted a finger for silence, read for a few more moments, then snapped shut the book. "What do you want, Harry?"

"I was thinking the fine company of a friend, but from that tone, it seems there is no fine company to be had."

Merry stood and brushed down her skirt. "Forgive me, I was determined to finish that chapter. The housekeeper has insisted that every ounce of silverware must be polished today and there wasn't a single room that was not occupied."

Harcourt looked over at the house, nestled in a dip between the gentle rolling hills. Though smaller than his own house, Whitely was probably the second finest home in Dorset with elegant cream columns and squared off corners that left one in no doubt money had been spent on the design and creation. It was hard to imagine there was not a single room left unoccupied, but he knew Merry could not bear the slightest disturbance when studying.

"It's too nice a day to be inside anyway." He looked pointedly at her book. "Or to be reading."

"What do you have against reading?" She clutched the book to her chest as though he might have hurt the damned book's feelings.

"I have nothing against reading. You know I enjoy a good book or two. But not *all* the time. You should put your books down occasionally, Merry, and experience the world a little more."

She sniffed dismissively. "I don't see what the world has to offer me that cannot be found in a book."

"You would rather be spending time with Greek gods, is that not it? Us mere mortals aren't good enough for you."

"I like some mere mortals, but you must admit, there are many who leave something to be desired."

He chuckled. "I will concur. But not everyone is so awful. If you would but spend a little more time socializing, you would see that."

She gave a mock shudder. "I'd rather spend time with Mrs. Kemp while she polishes every piece of silverware in existence than...socialize." She said the word as though it created a bitter taste in her mouth.

He shook his head. "Merry, you are not an old spinster aunt. Do not speak as though you are. You should be dancing at balls and visiting the opera."

She peered at him over her glasses. "Opera is overrated. And you know I loathe dancing."

"Only because you have not found the right partner yet." He met her gaze directly and let his lips curve.

Scowling a little, she eyed him back then blinked. "You do know Daniel is not returning for at least another month?"

He smiled. "I do indeed. Am I not allowed to call upon you?"

"You are, but I know very well why you are calling upon me. You have been doing this almost every week since you returned from London. Do you not have some important estate work to see to or a widow in London to seduce?"

Inwardly, he grimaced. It had been a long time since he had seduced a widow and while he did not particularly regret his younger years, he regretted Merry knew about it all. After all, how was he ever to change her mind about him, if she thought him a complete rake?

He opted for ignoring the comment. "I am completely at your service."

"Well, I do not need you at my service, Harry. I can look after myself whether Daniel thinks so or not."

"Daniel knows you can look after yourself. I, however, am not so certain."

She glared at him, her lips turning into a mutinous pout. Her mouth, narrow but full, was always this stunning, almost berry red color. It made it damnably hard to concentrate on other things when he spoke to her.

"I am a grown woman in case you have forgotten, I am completely capable of being without my father or brother for a while."

Oh, he hadn't forgotten. Not one bit. How could he when she was standing in front of him, arms crossed under her breasts, reminding him of that enticingly curved figure that seemed to have come from nowhere a few years ago. She glared at him, her lips still pursed, her freckled nose thrusting upward. How little Merry had always hated being treated like a child.

"Completely capable, yes, but you do have a propensity for mischief."

"What some call mischief, I call simply living life. But, of course, when a lady does anything even slightly different, it is called mischief." She pointed her delicate nose in the air. "Anyway, it has been a long time since I have become embroiled in mischief."

He grinned. "So you agree you are a mischief."

"No...it's just that..." She huffed. "Must you always tease me?"

"Always." He let his smile broaden. "Do not forget I knew little Merry, who would hide from her governess and let the poor woman search for hours until she was in tears."

She opened her mouth to protest then snapped it shut and folded her arms. "The woman could not teach me anything I could not learn from books. She did not even like Homer!"

Harcourt chuckled. The thought that someone might not enjoy Merry's reading tastes was beyond her. "What about the various balls, where you and your friends would dash off to hide and drink sherry instead?"

"Sherry is far more interesting than stuffy old men who want to step on my toes."

"Am I a stuffy old man?"

"Did you ever wish to dance with me?" she countered.

He had no retort for that. For his sins, he had not been interested. Merry was his friend's little sister and a good acquaintance at best. At least until recently. Now...now she was so much more.

"I know you detest being interrupted when you're reading, Merry, but I had hoped for a warmer welcome than this."

She rolled her eyes, but her defensive position eased. "I cannot invite you in with Father and Daniel away."

"I know." He motioned toward a pillared folly. "If we cannot enjoy tea together, shall we walk instead? You can update me on your Greek translations."

Her book clutched at her side, she led the way across the wild grassland that was separated from the more formal gardens by way of a long line of hedges and tall trees.

"We shall be out of site of the house here. Mrs. Kemp does not approve of your visits without Daniel being here."

"Mrs. Kemp does not approve of much."

Merry giggled. "Why do you think I come out here to work? Mrs. Kemp is a fine housekeeper but why she thinks she can mother me I do not know. She is forever insisting I should be doing more ladylike things than reading or studying."

"Like embroidery or playing the piano I suppose?"

She gave a faux yawn. "You have heard my piano playing. It leaves a lot to be desired."

He nodded. "Indeed it does. Perhaps that is why Mrs. Kemp wishes you to practice."

"I could practice for one hundred years and get no better. Some people are not meant to play piano, and I am definitely one of them. I am afraid I will forever disappoint poor Mrs. Kemp."

"Well, you never disappoint me, Merry. Even if you are terrible at the piano."

"Well, I—" She stopped and peered into the distance.

Looking in the same direction, he spotted a rider making haste down the main road to the house. From his livery and pace, it was an urgent message.

"Perhaps it is from Daniel," said Merry, slightly breathless.

A knot fisted in his gut. There could be few reasons for an urgent message—and none of them good.

"Come, let us see what he wants." Harcourt led the way across the grass to the house. They caught up with the rider by the time he reached the front of the house.

The man dismounted and held a letter aloft. "Urgent message for Lord Daniel Bradford."

Merry sucked in a breath. "That's my brother. He is away from home. I'll take it."

Harcourt paid the man a tip while Merry tore open the letter and scanned the paper.

"Oh." Her knees buckled, and Harcourt had to act quickly to wrap an arm about her and support her.

"What is it?"

She peered up at him, her eyes wide with shock. "It's Father. He—he's dead."

Chapter Two

Merry sagged onto a chair and peered around the drawing room. It was growing late but the summer sun had yet to give itself up. However, the room seemed gray and dull. She stared at the empty fireplace. The clock on the mantelpiece ticked—louder than normal it seemed. A creak of floorboards indicated servants still lingered outside the room, even though she had dismissed them.

She was in no mood to be around people, not now everyone had dispersed after the funeral. Fingering the fabric of her black gown, she considered the strange, empty feeling inside her. Nothing was different—not really. Her father was rarely at home anyway. Him being dead made little difference to her life.

And yet...

She tried to swallow the knot in her throat.

Her family had done their best to comfort her. Which had been strange. She didn't need comfort. She had never really felt anything for her father. He was a stranger to her. She'd been raised by nannies and a governess who never quite knew what to do with her.

Then Daniel had taken over the role of her protector. Father had just been someone who shut himself away in his office for a while before brusquely saying farewell and going away again.

Merry touched her cheek with gloved hands. She could not even recall if he had ever embraced her or brushed a fatherly kiss across her forehead.

She tugged off the gloves and flung them over the side of the chair. Her stays were pulling too tight and a headache had begun to form where the pins pulled her hair too tight. As she plucked them out one by one, the drawing room door eased open.

"I said—" She paused when she realized it was not a servant. "Harry! I thought you had left."

The Earl of Langley stepped fully into the room. "I should have done perhaps." He eased the door shut. "But I could not bring myself to."

Merry stood. "You need not worry. I am perfectly well." She forced a smile.

He stepped toward her. She had always been aware Harcourt was terribly handsome. The extensive line of lovers he left in his wake was a testament to that. But there was something about him in his funeral wear that had her breath catching slightly. It was an odd sensation—one she had never experienced around Harry before. She pressed a hand to her stomach.

"Are you well? Do you feel faint?"

She suspected she must look horribly pale. With Daniel away, arranging the funeral had been left up to her. Thankfully she had excellent servants who had helped her with most of it. The butler had been particularly useful. But she had never had to consider such things before. What hymns they would they sing? What the coffin would look like? What would be engraved on her father's headstone? It has left her feeling strung out and older than her years.

"I am well." She kept the smile in place. "Go home, Harry. You should not be here anyway."

"No one is around, and if a man cannot comfort his friend in a time of need, then to hell with everyone."

A slight laugh bubbled out of her. It was not because he was being especially funny, but his determined expression was a welcome relief from the concerned looks everyone kept giving her.

"I'm glad you can still smile."

"Of course, I can still smile. I am just fine. Really, I am. You know father and I were not—" Her voice cracked. She gulped and tried again, aware her voice was reed thin. "Were not close."

"I know, but grief is a strange thing." He inched closer so that there was barely a foot between them. He tucked a curl behind her ear and the slight warmth of his fingers jarred straight to her heart.

"Daniel shall be home before long," she said brightly. "I have sent a message to Spain. Of course, it shall take some time to arrive, but I am certain that he shall want to hurry home as soon as he can. After all, he is the new viscount."

For some reason, Harry would not take his eyes off her. He kept staring at her as though searching for something. It made her feel like she needed to keep rabbiting on until he left or else he might spot something she did not wish him to see.

"He shall want to take up his position quickly and ensure the estate continues to run efficiently, I'm sure," she continued.

"He might be some time. If the weather is bad on the crossing, it could be weeks before he returns," he cautioned.

"Of course. I will not expect him any time soon, though I must start getting ready for his return."

Turning away, she skimmed her hand across the back of the chaise and paused by the window. Outside, the estate sprawled in front of her. She would have to keep it running until Daniel returned—no easy feat. Though she understood how to keep the household going, estate affairs had been very much kept from her by her brother and father. Even when she'd expressed interest in learning, she'd been told there was no reason for her to know.

Well, she was nothing if not a quick learner, and her father had employed some of the best estate managers in the country. Surely it would not be too hard?

She sensed Harry moving closer, coming up behind her. He put a hand to her arm and she turned to face him.

"If you need any help, Merry, I intend to be around as much as you need me. I need to return to London briefly, but I will be staying in Lulworth for the whole of summer."

"And miss out on the social scene? That does not sound like you." She tried to add a little amusement into her tone but if fell flat.

"There are more important things than socializing."

"That definitely does not sound like you."

"Merry, I would not leave you in a time of need."

Merry peered up at him. She wanted to protest that statement but could not bring herself to. He'd discarded his hat somewhere, though she had not noticed where, and his chestnut hair had a slightly mussed look to it. She'd always thought of his green eyes as soulful and far too pretty for a man but now she almost hated him for them. They were too intrusive, too aware of everything that was wrapping itself about her insides. How could he know that deep down she was about to break?

Somehow...just somehow Harcourt Easton knew her inside out.

The knot in her throat bunched tighter and her eyes burned. When she felt the first tear escape, she crumbled. A sob bubbled out of her followed by another then another.

Harry closed the gap and wrapped his arms around her, bringing her into the warm cocoon of his embrace. She pressed her face into his chest while great sobs wracked her. She could not be sure how long the painful, ugly tears consumed her, but at some point, she became aware of Harry's hands rubbing up and down her back.

"I do not..." She sucked in a breath but kept her face against his warm, solid chest. "I do not even know why I am crying. I did not love him. And I am certain he did not love me."

He didn't say anything, just kept up the soothing touch of his palms over her back.

"I suppose I wonder what might have been...what could have happened if we'd had more time. Maybe one day he would have taken the time to get to know me...maybe..." Another ripple of emotion welled out of her and she could not bring herself to hold it back. She cried until there was nothing left in her.

As the sobs eased, Harry maneuvered her to the chaise longue and eased her down with him. Her eyes were sore and itchy from tears and her chest burned. She found herself scooped up and laid across his lap, his arms enfolding her, making her feel warmer and more protected than she'd felt in days.

"I do wish he could have loved me," she spilled out.

Harry cupped her head against his chest. She could hear his steady heartbeat, heavy and reassuring. His legs were firm underneath her and she felt the flex of muscles in his arms as he held her tight. For a moment, just for a moment, she allowed herself to be taken away by the feeling. Considering she had recently declared she had no need for men, she could not let herself relish it too much, but there was something wonderfully comforting about having a strong, confident man taking away her worries—if briefly.

"He should have loved you, Merry," Harry murmured. "There is so much about you to love."

She wasn't so sure. Daniel loved her, to be certain, but in that brotherly sort of 'what is Merry up to now' way. Since an early age, she'd always been determined to do her own thing. Her governess could not keep up with her and eventually let her manage her own lessons. Stubbornness and being a little too know-it-all at times were not qualities people loved.

"I understand why he did not," she whispered, feeling another trickle of tears run down her face.

"Well, I do not." He eased her back a little so that he could lift her chin with a finger and look into her eyes. "There is so much about you to love," he repeated firmly. "If your father could not see that, that is his fault, and not yours. You are guilty of nothing more than being yourself."

"Perhaps I should not have been myself...perhaps I should have been better...nicer...more dutiful..." Inwardly, she cursed the tears that would not seem to stop coming. They blurred her vision and trickled down her nose.

Harry drew a handkerchief out of his pocket and dabbed away the tears. He brushed a finger along her cheek.

"It was your father who should have done better, not you. Now you must pick yourself up and be the stubborn, strong-headed Merry we all know and love."

Merry sniffed.

"I mean it." He tucked that finger back under her chin.

She nodded slowly, meeting his gaze. Her stomach did a little flip while his gaze searched hers. She could see the tiny creases around his mouth and eyes and the little brown flecks in the green surrounding his pupils. His pupils widened, darkening his eyes.

Harry leaned down and pressed his lips to hers. They were warm and gentle. Her heart came to a standstill. Before she knew what she was doing, she was kissing him back. The gentleness gave rapidly away to a passionate sweep of his tongue. Her body tingled from head to toe and her mind was a whirl. She gripped his neck and willed the kiss to never end.

Unfortunately, he pulled back, she felt as though his lips had to still be there, lingering over her mouth. Merry fought for something to say, for her body to move...for anything...but Harcourt Easton had kissed her—what on earth was she meant to do?

He gave a soft smile and eased her off onto the chaise. Pressing the handkerchief into her palm, he dropped a second kiss to her forehead. "Have your lady's maid fill up a bath and be sure to eat something warm," he ordered as he straightened.

She nodded numbly.

"I have to go to London for a few days, but I'll be back, and I expect to find you with your head buried in books and telling me off as usual."

She nodded again.

He seemed to hesitate then change his mind. "Never change, Merry, you are perfect the way you are."

When the door thudded shut behind him, it seemed to snap her back. She stared down at the handkerchief and rubbed her fingers across the initials stitched carefully into it. Drawing in a breath, she sat up. Harry was right—but she would never admit as much. There was no changing the past and at the age of twenty, there was no changing her. If her father could not love her, that was not her fault. Now she needed to focus on the future.

And not on that kiss.

Fingers to her lips, she frowned. She had known Harcourt for most of her life, and they had been friends since she came out into Society. He'd taken her hand and even danced with her on occasion, but he'd never kissed her. She supposed she had never been grieving before either. Perhaps it was his way of comforting her. After all, he was such a rake, kissing women for any reason whatsoever was probably quite normal to him.

Not to her, however. That could safely be considered her first kiss, and she had certainly never expected it to come from Harry. No matter how handsome and wonderful she thought him, soon-to-be spinsters did not expect kisses from veritable rakes.

She sighed and smoothed her hands down her skirts. Better not to tell the Spinster Club about it, though. They would never understand why a male friend had kissed her.

Chapter Three

When Harcourt threw down his cards, Griff shot him a look.

Harcourt glowered at him. "What is it?"

"You're not even trying." Griff gathered up the cards and his winnings and slid them back into his pocket.

"I am having a run of bad luck."

Griff shook his head and signaled to the waiter with an empty glass. Two fresh brandies arrived promptly. Harcourt eyed the liquid then the now empty table. Griff was right of course. He had little interest in cards. He'd come to Boodles out of habit and what a pointless habit it was. If Merry were here she'd tell him to do something constructive like write a letter or read a new book. As far as he was concerned, he'd leave the books to her, but spending night after night in gentlemen's clubs was growing thin.

Smoke clouded the air of the grand building, mingling with the scent of leather and whisky. Once upon a time, he'd loved nothing more than sitting in these clubs with his friends, drinking the night away and besting them all at poker or whist.

"I am merely contemplating my return to Dorset," he explained. "My business here is settled."

Griff made a dismissive noise. "What the devil will you do in Dorset for the summer? You cannot beat London for fine clubs and even finer women." He leaned in. "Do not tell me a woman has turned you down and you are running away with your tail between your legs?"

Harcourt gave him a look. Everyone knew he had no problems with women, and he'd enjoyed the company of many a fine lady these past years. But, again, the endless stream of women in his bed had grown tiresome. They were strong, independent women who needed nothing more from him than a quick tumble, but since he had turned thirty, his desire for such dalliances had declined. He'd rather argue with a woman under a tree than bed a practical stranger again.

Michael Griffin, heir to the Dukedom of Harington, wouldn't understand one jot. If Harcourt was considered a rake, who knew what Griff was? But with his father alive and kicking, Griff hardly felt the need to settle down any time soon, and Harcourt could not see him ever being tamed, even once marriage was needed.

"You need a new conquest," Griff declared. He drained his drink and slammed the glass down. "Come on, Easton, there's a party at Lady Seville's. Let us go there and find you some company. That shall stir you out of..." He waved a hand. "Whatever this is."

Harcourt threw back his brandy and pictured the party. There would be dancing and drink. Lots of young ladies vying for a husband, and a few widows or older women looking for an experienced lover who could fulfill the needs that their husbands neglected.

He shook his head. "I think I shall head home."

"Lady Bambridge will be there."

Harcourt scowled, trying to recall the lady. Glossy black hair and voluptuous figure came to mind.

"She has implied she wishes to spend time in your company again," Griff confided, his brows wagging.

Shaking his head, Harcourt stood. "I think my bed is calling."

His friend blinked at him. "Do I need to call a doctor?"

Harcourt chuckled. "Because I have turned down one ball?"

"Because you have not been the same roguish Harcourt I know for some time now. But this...this is even worse. Going to bed alone? You must be ill indeed." Griff paused and frowned. "You're not dying, are you?"

Harcourt chuckled. "No, I am not dying. I simply wish for my bed. But you enjoy the rest of your night. If Lady Bambridge is that keen for a lover, I'm sure you will do admirably." He grinned. "Though she may find you a little disappointing compared to me."

Griff snorted. "Unlikely."

"Enjoy your evening."

Harcourt collected his hat and gloves and left the smoke and whisky fumes behind. Not that the streets of London smelled much better. It used to be that he could not wait to draw in the smoky smell of Town as opposed to the clear air of Lulworth. After his education at Oxford, he'd spent as much time in London as possible, taking every advantage afforded to him. For almost a decade, he'd gambled, drank, danced, and bedded his way through Town.

He approached a hansom cab and instructed the driver to take him home. Once he climbed into the carriage, he tugged out his pocket watch. Ten o'clock. Early indeed for a gentleman about town. He didn't regret calling it an early night, though. The sooner he went to bed, the sooner he could rise and quit London. The thought of fresh smelling air and grass beneath his feet appealed far more than sweaty bodies in a ballroom and warm punch.

He snapped the watch shut and shoved it back into his pocket. Of course, it was Merry that was the real appeal. He shouldn't have left her. He'd thought perhaps giving her space would help and he did need to meet with his accountant—though of course the accountant was paid quite enough to come to him. Leaving her had been a mistake, he realized that now.

Just as he had realized many other things recently. Namely that he was getting too old to be a rake. His mother had been pestering him to settle down ever since he'd inherited his earldom eight years ago, but he'd had little interest in doing so. He had now come to understand it was because he had not found the right woman yet. Or to be more accurate, he had not appreciated that the right woman was there—right in front of him. The girl he'd come to consider a fine friend had become a remarkable young woman—and he was no longer interested in being a rake.

The carriage rolled to a halt and he pressed a hand to the door to steady himself. After paying the driver, he raced up the steps to the townhouse and barged inside. His valet attended to him quickly with a raise of a brow.

"You're early, my lord."

"Yes." Harcourt glanced round the quiet entranceway as he shrugged off his jacket. "Are any of the maids still around?"

Harlow nodded. "If you are hungry—-"

He shook his head. "No, I need my belongings packed at once. We are leaving. Tonight."

A crease marred Harlow's forehead. "Tonight, my lord? But it is far too late to travel."

"I wasn't making a suggestion."

A knock at the door preventing the valet from protesting further. Harcourt yanked open the door to find Griff on the doorstep.

"What the devil are you doing here?" asked Harcourt.

Griff grinned. "Coming to see what all the fuss is about?"

"Fuss?" Harcourt scowled and stepped back to allow his friend to enter. "Harlow, rouse the maids. I wish to leave now."

Harlow stomped off upstairs, muttering about how the maids would have his balls for this. Harcourt turned his attention back to Griff.

"Did you not have a party to attend to?"

Griff gave a shrug. "I could do with a change of scenery. And I have a hankering to see what it is that draws you home with such haste. Especially when it has been occupying your attention for quite some time of late."

"Dorset will bore you to tears."

Griff leaned against the doorframe with practiced insouciance. With black hair and a profile ruined—or perhaps not in the eyes of many women—by a broken nose from his early years, Griff's every move was practiced, carefully honed to ensure he had full impact. Why the devil the man felt the need to use it on him, Harcourt did not know. He'd known Griff almost as long as he'd known Merry's brother, and he was no simpering virgin just begging to be seduced by the infamous Lord Michael Griffin.

"I have nothing to do so why not take the country air?"

"Griff." Harcourt pinched the bridge of his nose. "I have enough to do on the estate without worrying about entertaining you."

Griff's smile widened, a flash of white in the darkened corridor of the house. "I can entertain myself, I am sure. A bonny country lass would make a pleasant change."

Curling a hand at his side, Harcourt forced himself to take a breath. Griff would not go near Merry if he told his friend of how he felt, but he'd be damned if he was willing to admit as much yet. The man would revel in it and most certainly get in the way. If he was to win Merry, he'd have to do it alone.

And after that kiss, he had no doubt she felt the same. Whether the stubborn Merry would be willing to admit as much, he did not know. But he'd felt it down to his soul and seen it in her eyes.

Perhaps now was not the best time, and he'd intended to give her more space to grieve—really he had—but staying away from her was eating away inside of him. He felt empty and hollow.

Footsteps and a few muttered curse words echoed around upstairs. With any luck, Harlow would have him packed and ready to leave within the hour. He could reach Dorset by dawn and see how Merry was after breakfast.

He glanced at Griff who remained against the doorframe with clearly little intention to move. Harcourt sighed.

"Fine, but if you cause any scandal, I shall disavow all knowledge of our friendship."

Griff straightened. "Excellent. You need someone to keep you on the right path. Something odd is going on with you, Easton. I just know it."

"If the right path means following in your footsteps, I am not at all sure I want to remain on it."

Griff shook his head sadly. "See? This is what I mean? Once upon a time, you'd have been next to me on that path. Hell, sometimes you were ahead of me. Whatever has caused this change has something to do with that little village of yours and I intend to find out what it is."

"Nothing has caused this change, Griff. It's simply called growing up. You might like to try it some time."

"Pfft. Never. I shall remain the same always."

Harcourt chuckled. "We shall see."

Chapter Four

Merry tilted her head and eyed the spines of the books in front of her. An array of red, green, and blue leather, each lettered with gold spanned the entire wall in front of her. She sighed and turned to Mr. Jameson. "No new titles then?"

The shopkeeper shook his head. "You know I would tell you if there were, Lady Merry. Every time I visit London, I inquire for you."

"I know." She tried not to sigh again but she had been hoping that there was at least one book on Greek myths she had not read yet. Almost monthly, she visited the book shop in the center of the village in the hopes there might be something.

"You should read slower, my lady," Mr. Jameson teased, his eyes creasing in the corners. "Or find another topic you feel so passionately about."

"I know," she repeated.

Her obsession with all things Greek had started as a child when she had run away from her governess and picked up a book on Greek myths. The adventure, the romance, the magic...it had all swept her away. It was not that she never read anything else, but nothing quite took her away from the world like those myths did.

"I shall be in London again soon, so I shall make some further inquiries," he informed her. "We shall find you something new to read, don't you worry."

She smiled at the old man who had been selling her books since she was a little girl. "Thank you, Mr. Jameson. You are too good to me."

"I cannot have my favorite customer disappointed now, can I, my lady?"

Before she could reply, the bell above the door rang and Arabella, Sophia, and Bella barreled into the shop.

"Not more books!" Bella rolled her eyes. "You have enough." She reached for her hand. "Good day, Mr. Jameson," she trilled before dragging her out of the shop. "Books are not what you need right now."

Merry tugged her hand from Bella's and folded her arms. "What do you mean by that?"

"I mean, you do not need to be tucking yourself away and reading. You need to be spending time with friends—"

"Is that not precisely what I am doing now?" Merry motioned to her three friends who had gathered in a circle around her.

"What Sophia is trying to say"—Arabella cut in—"is that we want to make sure you are well, and that perhaps some fresh air might do you some good."

Merry uncrossed her arms and glanced around at the concerned faces. It had been a week since she'd buried her father and she had to admit she had not exactly been sociable. There had been a lot for her to mull over. But the strange empty feeling had already begun to ease. She was sorry he was dead and sorry they never had the relationship she had hoped for, but she had hers and Daniel's future to think of now.

"You do not need to worry for me, I promise," she assured them all. "I am a little numb to it perhaps, but I am well. I am not brooding, I promise."

Arabella hooked her arm through Merry's and they started down the main road of the village. Set back from the cliff edges and tucked between two hills, Lulworth consisted of mostly thatched cottages. Several of them were home to shops and at the end of the long road that dissected the village was a sizeable inn. For those who like London or Bath, it had little to offer, but for Merry, it was perfect. Her friends thought so too. Here they could avoid worrying about whether they would run into anyone important and what they would do if they did. None of them enjoyed those sorts of interactions.

"I am determined to be moved into the dower house before Daniel returns," Merry explained as they strolled down the road in a row. "If he is to be taking on the title, he will have a lot to deal with and he does not need to be worrying about me or whether the dower house is ready."

Arabella frowned. "There's so much work to be done, though. Surely you would be better off waiting until he returns? Have you even looked inside the house recently? What if there are...I don't know...holes in the roof?"

Chuckling, Merry shook her head. "I think it is quite sound, just a little dirty and unloved."

"That sounds like Bella after she's been tending to the pigs!" Sophia said.

Bella thrust out her tongue. "I shall have you know the pigs love me very much."

"They're the only ones who will," Sophia teased.

"I did not come out here to be insulted. I thought we were here to support Merry." Bella gave Sophia a gentle shove, sending her a few steps sideways.

Sophia nudged her back, knocking her into Arabella and then into Merry.

"Careful!!" Arabella exclaimed as she steadied herself.

"Do not forget that we have vowed to go without men," Merry reminded them.

"Yes, we vowed not to marry them, but that does not mean we cannot ask them for help," pointed out Arabella.

"Oh look, new bonnets!" Bella pointed toward the drapers.

They headed over and peered into the shop window. An array of new bonnets were indeed displayed. Feathered monstrosities and large brimmed hats filled the display, all in bright gaudy colors. Merry grimaced. "It looks as though Mrs. Bryce has been shopping again."

Sophia nodded. "She always thinks she has the best taste in fashion."

"Let us go try some on." Bella darted into the shop before any of them could protest. Rolls of fabric were laid out on the center table and lined the shelves. Ribbons hung from above. Bella snatched up the biggest, ugliest bonnet she could find and plopped it on her head before posing. "What do you think?"

"Hideous," Sophia said. "What was Mrs. Bryce thinking?" she murmured. "These are her worst yet."

Bella picked up a wide-brimmed froth of lace and straw and dunked it on Merry's head. "This looks like it was made for you."

Merry almost staggered under the weight of the thing. She blew away a piece of lace that hung in front of her eye and tried to adjust it. She crossed her eyes. "I can hardly see out from underneath it!"

"Oh, but it does suit you so well." Arabella giggled.

"It really does, my lady." Mrs. Bryce stepped out from the rear room and Merry winced at her beatific expression. Round and short, Mrs. Bryce always dressed in what she considered to be the most fashionable clothes. Her color choices were never quite right, however, and always clashed with the perpetual ruddiness in her face.

Mrs. Bryce flicked her gaze over Merry. "It does not go so well with your mourning wear, but you should purchase it nonetheless. It will be something to look forward to wearing."

"Oh, I do not think—" Merry paused, not quite willing to crush the woman's hopeful expression. "Well, I suppose it would not hurt to own another bonnet. But I do think Bella should purchase hers as well, do you not think, Mrs. Bryce?"

A slight gasp emanated from Bella. Merry gave her a smug look.

The woman's smile broadened. "I do indeed. You look quite well in that, Miss Bella." Mrs. Bryce tilted her head "Almost...pretty."

"Almost pretty," Bella hissed. "What a compliment. If that bonnet makes me look almost pretty, I must be ugly indeed."

Merry knew Bella considered herself untraditional. Her strong features were not what was fashionable but that did not make her ugly at all. It didn't seem to matter how many times they told her that, though. Bella always dismissed their compliments and told them she did not care if she were the ugliest woman in the world. Merry was not so sure that was true.

Once they had paid for their bonnets, Bella snatched Merry's and shoved it back on her head. "She needs to wear it right now, do you not think, Mrs. Bryce? It will make her feel so much better."

Merry gave her friend's ankle a tap with her boot and shot her a look.

"Indeed I do." Mrs. Bryce beamed at her. "It really does wonders for your complexion and you do not want to gain anymore freckles now, do you, my lady?"

Merry held back a sigh and thanked the shopkeeper. "As soon as we are out of sight, I am losing this bonnet," she muttered to Bella. "It's quite windy today, is it not? What a shame it would be if it blew away into the sea."

"Look how happy you made her, though," Bella said, glancing back.

"I know." She glanced back at Mrs. Bryce who had hustled away and could be heard humming to herself even from the door. Merry supposed she had at least done her good deed for the day.

As she pushed open the door, she tumbled into a chest—a strong, masculine chest that spanned her vision. She tried to peer up at the owner of the chest, but the ridiculous breadth of the bonnet prevented her from seeing anything but his cravat. She'd recognize that chuckle anywhere though.

"New bonnet?"

Merry divested herself of the thing immediately, clasping it in one hand. Harry smiled down at her and her stomach did that strange flip thing again. In shining hessians, breeches that clung to his thighs, and an elegantly embroidered navy waistcoat, he looked far more fashionable than she ever would, even without the bonnet.

She glanced at the man next to him who was dressed just as finely and had black hair and a blue gaze that was so bright and curious that she looked away immediately. "Um, yes." Merry bit down on her lip and peered at her friends who were huddled behind her.

"It's a little on the large side."

She chuckled. "That is putting it tactfully. When did you get back?"

"Last night." He motioned to his companion. "Please let me introduce my friend, Lord Thornford."

"Oh, he's the son of the Duke of Harington," Bella hissed behind her, non-too-subtly.

Lord Thornford's lips quirked. "A pleasure to meet you all. Please call me Griff."

"Um. What brings you to Dorset, Lord, um, Griff?" asked Sophia.

"I wanted to see this wonderful village that Easton always talks about. I can see why he was eager to return home." His gaze ran across all the women as he grinned.

Merry saw the color in her friends' cheeks. It was not often they had a stranger in their midst, particularly spectacularly handsome ones, but they had to be as aware as she was that the rumors surrounding the Duke of Harington's son were far worse than those surrounding Harry.

"How are you?" Harry asked her.

The concern in his eyes made her feel strangely soft inside. She found her gaze kept falling to his lips while she recalled how soft and warm they had been. By some miracle, she'd managed to forget that kiss. Until now. Until they were surrounded by their friends and he was right in front of her. She'd managed to convince herself she'd practically made it up, that it had been the chaste kiss of a concerned friend and that it did not light feelings that she had long suppressed.

"I..." Those feelings that were currently frothing forth, blanking her mind and making it impossible to say a word.

"She's going to move into the dower house soon," Bella spilled out. "Before Daniel returns."

"Yes, thank you, Bella," Merry said tightly.

Harry's brows lifted. "The dower house? It's a bit of a wreck, is it not?"

"I always intended to move there once Daniel returned, but I think it necessary to move before he comes home. He will have enough to be worrying about without having to set up my home," she explained.

"And let me guess, you intend to do it all alone." His lips curved.

"Well, not exactly..." Merry huffed. "I can manage you know. I am not completely helpless."

He lifted a hand. "I would never imply such a thing, but if you need some help, I would be more than happy to lend a hand."

"As would I," offered Lord Thornford.

Merry shook her head vigorously. If he made her stomach flip simply by standing in front of her, she could not bear to have him helping her at the house.

"It might be useful..." Arabella started.

Merry shook her head again. "I'll manage. My friends are going to help, are you not, ladies?"

Glances swung between them and they eventually all nodded.

"Um, yes, of course." Arabella twined her hands together and color bloomed on her cheeks. Merry resisted the desire to roll her eyes. Arabella was the worst fibber, she really was.

Harcourt's lips quirked. "Well, I shall like to see how things are coming along anyway. I shall see you soon, Merry. Have a good day, ladies."

Lord Thornford bid them farewell with a tip of his hat, and both men strode down the street. Merry watched their confident walk as did her friends. Once he vanished, she eyed Bella.

"You did not need to tell him about the house, you know."

Bella held up her hands. "I did not think it was some great secret. Besides, I thought you considered Lord Easton your friend. Why should he not know?"

"Because well...well..." Because he had kissed her. Because it felt strange. Because she was scared that she might want another kiss. This was not how it was meant to be. Sophia was right, Harry was her brother's friend—and nothing more. He had kissed her to comfort her, and she was a fool to think anything more of it.

"You should have accepted his help, Merry," said Arabella. "You could probably clear the house in half the time with a strong man to help."

"And Lord Harcourt Easton is certainly strong," giggled Sophia.

"So is Lord Thornford," added Bella. "*So* strong."

"Have you forgotten everything we said?" snapped Merry. "No men. We made vows!"

"Yes, not to marry them. It does not mean we cannot admire a muscle or two," Sophia said saucily. "If you had once been married to a dry old stick of a man, you might wish to admire muscles too."

Merry pressed her lips together and tried not to laugh. How Sophia had ever survived a marriage to such a man, she did not know, but she was grateful she had come out of the match with her sense of humor intact.

"No matter how muscular a man is, we do not need them," Merry determined. "We shall fix the dower house ourselves. We do not need men."

Chapter Five

Like a miniature version of the main house, the dower house had tall windows and square proportions. Two grand pillars marked the front door. Harcourt paused and peered up at the building with a shake of his head. Ivy clung to one side, crawling its way up to block out the light of one of the upper windows.

Even from here he could see that the windows were cloudy with grime and dust. The building had been neglected since the death of Merry's great-grandmother—long before Merry was born. If he didn't know Merry better, he'd think her ridiculous for taking on such a project but, of course, Merry could tackle most things she put her mind to.

The front door was slightly ajar, so he pushed it open and stepped inside. Griff had decided to remain abed, for which he was grateful. Griff was a good friend, but he'd already started coming to his own conclusions about the local ladies and he did not need his friend interfering—especially when he knew he'd be horrified Harcourt had decided now was the time to take the path to matrimony.

The scent of dust and mildew greeted him. Underfoot there were tiles that had once been red but were lost under a sheet of dust. He glanced into the two rooms to either side where furniture lay under white sheets but saw no sign of Merry. A creak from upstairs made him pause, and then the slightly out of tune humming made him smile. At least the stairs looked in good condition. The large oak staircase that led all the way up the center of the hallway would need a little cleaning and that was about it. Harcourt headed up and followed the sound of humming.

He found Merry in one of the bedrooms. Sheets covered all the furniture here too. She wore gray and black, but the gown had been marred by streaks of dirt. Her curls were a wild array with several escaping down her neck and clouding around her head. Her humming meant she didn't hear him approach as she stared up at a disconcerting hole in the ceiling.

"Merry." His voice echoed around the room.

"Oh." She whirled, her foot catching on a floorboard as she did.

Harcourt leaped forward and caught her as she tumbled forward. She pushed herself up and away from him, a little color staining her cheeks.

"You startled me."

He gave a rueful smile. "Forgive me. I called at the house, but they said you were here."

"I thought it was about time I started work."

He swung his gaze about the room. "There's a lot to do."

She straightened. "I can manage."

His lips quirked. So defensive, so damned stubborn. It was one of the things he loved about her. He'd been raised by a strong woman and had come to appreciate such qualities. There was no tougher woman than Merry, though. Her intellect had always set her apart from others and had made her seem odd to many. Being a viscount's daughter and being 'odd' was no easy task, but she'd survived it admirably.

"How exactly are you going to fix a hole in the ceiling?"

She glanced back at the hole and sighed. "Well, I have other things to worry about first. Follow me." She led him into what must have once been another room but was now cluttered with furniture, paintings, vases and books, as well as endless curiosities. "I think someone used this house as storage for the big house at some point," she explained. "I had no idea we even owned this many...things. This is not even the only room like this. The other bedroom is full, as well as one of the drawing rooms downstairs."

"What will you do with it all?"

She shrugged. "I'm not certain. I cannot sell any of it as it all belongs to Daniel now, but I could move some of it to the attics at the house. And some of the furnishings could be used here." She patted a chair, sending up a cloud of dust that tickled the back of Harcourt's throat.

"Some of it is quite nice underneath all the dirt." A sneeze exploded from her and Merry fished a handkerchief out of her sleeve.

The embroidery on it caught his gaze and he allowed himself a small smile. It was the one he had given her. She'd kept it then. That had to mean something.

"You're going to need help, especially if you want to make this house livable before Daniel returns." He paused. "It's the curse isn't it?"

She wrinkled her nose. "How do you know about the curse?"

"Dan and I are friends if you recall. I think he brought it up one drunken night. Gave us all a good laugh."

"Well, if you must know, it is not about the curse. I just wish to give them some space. They are newlyweds, Harry, they deserve that much."

Harcourt snorted. "Few newlyweds get 'space' and most survive. This is about the curse." He grinned. "You think it might be true."

She sucked in a breath as though stunned he would even consider she might. "I certainly do not. Curses and magic and the like are entirely fictional. I would never believe such a thing."

"And yet you fear for Dan's marriage."

"Our family does not have the best record of successful marriages." Merry sighed. "We have yet to have a good one. I really hope Daniel's is the first. He deserves happiness."

"I have no doubt Isabel will make him happy indeed. You need not fear if your presence will hinder their match. And you certainly need not worry about this *curse*."

Her eyes narrowed at him. "I do not fear the curse," she insisted.

He turned and eyed the moldy ceiling above. "What will your brother think when he comes home and finds you have evacuated from the house?"

"I told him of my intentions before he left. He insisted it was not necessary but the more I think about it, the more it seems a sensible solution," she said matter-of-factly.

"Only you could think a young woman moving into a dower house alone is a sensible solution."

She pursed her lips. "Well I will not be completely alone. I shall have my maid and a servant or two with me. One of the kitchen maids has agreed to come and cook." A smile broke across her face. "I think I could be quite content here all alone. It shall give me plenty of time to study."

"There is more to life than studying."

An eyebrow rose. "Like drinking and gambling and dancing, I suppose."

"Like spending time with good friends." He moved closer.

He saw a slight tremble run through her body. She was not immune to him, he was certain of that. Admittedly kissing her after she had buried her father had not been his most sensible of moves but it had felt right at the time—a perfect way to comfort her. Pursuing her while she was in mourning might not even be the most gentlemanly of things to do either, but if her father's death had taught him anything, life was short. He had little intention of wasting anymore time.

"I'm not going to become a recluse simply because I move into this house, Harry."

"I know what you are like once you become lost in books. We shall be lucky to see you once a year," he teased.

"I must finish this translation."

"How long exactly will this translation take?"

"Oh years I suspect," she said breezily.

"Years? Christ, Merry. I thought the Odyssey had been translated already."

Hands to hips, she eyed him. "By men. All the translations have been done by men. And all translations are subject to bias. Because they are interpreted by men, they focus on the men, yet there are so many female characters of significant importance. I intend to translate it with the female view in mind."

Harcourt rubbed his forehead. "Well, if I know you at all, I am certain you shall do an outstanding job, but I'm sure sorting out this house—"

A crack sound rumbled through the house. He froze. Another cracking sound followed, and a sprinkling of plaster dusted Merry's nose. She wrinkled her nose and peered up. A sizable portion fell, this time landing on her head.

As the next rumbling of noise occurred, the ceiling gave way. Harcourt snatched Merry to him, hauling her to the door as a large lump of ceiling crashed down, cracking across the furniture. He eyed the great fragment of plaster and looked back at Merry. Plaster dust covered her face and smeared her mourning dress. Little fragments of white were stuck in her black hair.

She stared up at him, wide-eyed. He kept her close, aware of his heart pounding hard. Her lips parted, and he could swear he heard her deep breath in.

"Are you well?"

She nodded.

Her arms were slender beneath his touch. he was too aware of her figure even under her simple gown. Heat rolled through him like a storm breaching the skies. He saw her pulse flutter when he reached to pluck a fragment from her hair. Releasing one arm from his hold, he smoothed away the dust from her cheeks then her nose.

"You need to be more careful, Merry."

She nodded again. Her pale blue eyes had darkened. He had to mask a triumphant grin. She could not hide her reaction to him. Lady Merry Bradford desired him as much as he desired her. Now he just had to make her realize that she loved him too.

A final piece of ceiling landed with a crash. The sound seemed to wake her from the moment and she jerked away, much to his regret. Harcourt pushed a hand through his hair. He should just come out and say it, but he knew what Merry was like. She was so damned stubborn, she'd send him packing. He had to tread carefully. Make her see what he had. His time in London had secured it in his mind—he could not live life without her.

"I had better get back to work," she murmured, brushing her hands down her gown.

"I can help," he offered.

"No, I can manage." She kicked a lump of ceiling aside. "Do you not have your friend to entertain?"

"Griff is abed. And likely will be for a lot longer."

She pursed her lips. "He keeps London hours then."

Harcourt shrugged. "I suspect he shall realize the country is not for him within a few days and return. He seemed to think it would be interesting to visit Lulworth."

"We do not have wild parties and gentlemen's clubs, but I for one, rather appreciate that."

"As do I."

Her brows furrowed. "Not long ago, you could not wait to return to London. I distinctly remember you telling Daniel how much Lulworth bored you."

He could not recall the occasion, but it was likely several years ago. "Hmm, I do not remember saying as much, but a man can change his mind can he not?"

"His mind perhaps, but not his nature."

"Is there something wrong with my nature, Merry?"

She opened her mouth then shut it with a huff. "I really had better set to work."

"Very well. I shall visit again soon to see your progress."

"There's no need—"

"I'll see you soon, Merry." He grinned, and her cheeks flushed. He had her off-kilter and he could not help but like it. It meant she'd been as affected by their kiss as he. With any luck, she would not take much persuading before she recognized what was between them.

Chapter Six

"Achoo!" Bella fished a handkerchief out of her sleeve and dabbed her nose, grimacing. She dropped the sheet she was holding unceremoniously onto the floor. Another cloud of dust kicked about the drawing room and she sneezed again.

Arabella propped her hands on her hips and eyed her. "If you were a little more careful, it would be less dusty."

Merry fought to hold back a sneeze of her own. They had hardly done any work as yet and the room looked worse than ever. Dust swirled about in the afternoon sun that highlighted the mottled windows and streaks of dirt that lingered on everything. She had opted to clear one drawing room and one bedroom today, pointedly ignoring the one that was filled with *things* and a good deal of ceiling. If they could just get this room inhabitable, she would feel so much better about the idea.

Sophia kicked aside the pile of sheets and eyed the chairs they had uncovered. "Well, they could be worse..." She gave a shrug and glanced Merry's way.

Merry understood the look well enough. The chairs were threadbare and utterly out of fashion. Of course, she could not have expected them to be high-fashion given they had been hidden away for so long, but she had half-hoped for something elegant and timeless. These gaudy furnishings were another matter, however.

"Perhaps there are some good ones in storage," Arabella said brightly.

"I cannot imagine the best ones are hidden away," said Bella who received a jab in the ribs by Sophia's elbow.

Merry waved away the remark with a hand. "She is right."

"Do not lose hope." Coming to Merry's side, Arabella put a hand to her arm. "Perhaps there are some nice furnishings at the big house you can use."

Forcing a smile, Merry nodded. "Yes, I am sure there must be."

There were likely some unused chairs and other pieces tucked away in the cellars or attics of Whitely Grange. The problem was she would have to arrange someone to move them all over here. A cart would be needed and several people's time. Her staff—no her brother's staff—had enough to worry about at present. Juggling the running of the house and the estate along with trying to sort the dower house had kept Merry busier than she'd hoped. It had meant relying very much on all the servants and estate staff.

"Well, this house is not going to clean itself," Bella declared. "Let us open the windows and let some of the dust disperse while we take a look at that bedroom."

Merry's smile expanded. "Good idea."

At least she could rely on her friends to help. They had supported her through many things in her life, namely the awful balls and social events that left her feeling exhausted and awkward. Without them, she did not know how she would have managed her time in Society. She supposed once Daniel took the title, there might be expectations upon her once more but there was no chance Daniel would force her into anything.

"Thank you for helping," she said. "You can have little idea how much I appreciate it. I am desperately trying to keep the estate running efficiently and I will confess I am no expert."

Sophia nodded. "It must be quite a daunting task. With any luck, the weather shall be kind to Daniel and provide a quick crossing."

"I just hope he does not return home to an utter mess." Merry twined her hands together. "I can run a household well enough but the estate..." She sighed. "That's a different matter. My father nor Daniel allowed me any insight into it."

"You are the cleverest woman we know, Merry," Arabella told her. The others nodded. "I am sure you will be doing an excellent job and Daniel shall be so proud when he returns. Not only have you had to deal with your father's passing alone but you have had to take over a role you were never trained for."

"Why do you not just ask Harcourt for help?" Bella prompted. "He did offer it after all."

Sophia shot Bella a stern look. "Because we do not accept help from men, remember? Merry was quite firm about it."

Bella huffed. "You know I would rather have nothing to do with any man, especially with the amount of men I deal with on a daily basis." She rolled her eyes. "Just this morning my brothers were creating enough chaos to drive even the sanest woman mad. But Harcourt is a good man, is he not? And a fine friend to you."

"He might be a good man, but he is still a man." Besides, she could not quite bring herself to be in his company again so soon. Memories of being flat against him, feeling his muscles undulate under her fingertips were remarkably raw. She could hardly confess she had been reliving that moment again and again when alone after insisting on their vows. Her friends were relying on her to stay strong.

"He is a handsome man though," Arabella admitted softly.

"And he is a rake," Merry pointed out, even though the word sent a little pang of hurt to her chest.

It should not. It was something of which she'd been aware for a long time. It was widely acknowledged Harry had spent plenty of time with ladies in Society, thoroughly enjoying himself. Merry might not take a great interest in the gossip of the *ton* but there was no avoiding it sometimes.

"I heard that he has quit London for good." Bella grinned. "Perhaps he has found someone of interest here."

Merry held her breath. Surely they could not think...just because...no, it was all silly. Even if Harry truly was interested in her, it would be a strange sort of passing fancy. One she would be a fool for letting herself get involved in.

But none of that mattered! Her friends were relying on her to remain level-headed and support them in their vows. Particularly Arabella. Sophia and Bella did not seem to be quite so scarred by their experiences with men. The fact that Arabella had held onto her love for that rotten man for so long did not help. In the name of solidarity, she could not accept help from Harry.

"It does not matter what is keeping him here." Merry strode over to one of the windows and flicked the latches. "We do not need his help. We are four..." She tried to slide the window up. "Strong..." Pushing again with a grunt, she felt it shift a little. "Resourceful..." The window finally gave way, sliding up in one swift movement and sending her toppling backward. Arabella caught her, preventing her from falling to the floor. "Women," Merry finished, blowing a curl from her face and straightening. "Let us see what we can do upstairs."

Her friends dutifully marched upstairs, pausing to eye some of the rooms with gasps of horror. Merry led them into one of the master bedrooms. A four-poster bed dominated the room and what was likely a washstand sat under a cover. She had flung open the shutters on her last visit here, but the dark red color of the room made it appear smaller and more depressing than it should be. A large dresser had been abandoned in front of the bed for some reason and would need to be moved but apart from that, all they would have to do was give it a little clean.

"Well, this is...um..." Arabella bit down on her lip. "That is, I'm sure it shall be quite cozy once you have a fire in the grate."

Bella bent and peered into the fireplace. "You'll need a chimney sweep. If you light a fire in here, the whole house will go up." She straightened. "That might be a blessing."

Sophia shot her a look. "That was unkind."

Bella shrugged and giggled. "Well, at least all the dust would be gone."

Merry could not take offense at Bella's words. The work that needed to be done was overwhelming. She had never anticipated it being left in such poor condition. She'd considered that she'd have to move a few pieces of furniture around and lift off a couple of sheets originally. The option to get one or two of the maids to give the house a clean was still there but it would take several weeks of cleaning and none of them had that much time to spare. Merry did not even dare hire someone else, not when the estate was still in flux while waiting for her brother's return. All the money with the exception of her allowance and dowry was Daniel's and not hers to do with as she saw fit.

"Let us move this dresser, then we can take off the sheets and give everything a good dust down. I am certain it shall look just perfect once that is done." Merry managed to keep her tone bright but Bella still lifted a brow.

Sophia strode over to the dresser and grabbed one end. She grimaced. "It's heavy. Where shall we move it to?"

"I need it downstairs really. There is enough clutter in the bedrooms." Merry moved to the other end and gave it an experimental lift.

"We can probably manage that between us. It is not too large. Maybe if we remove the drawers, it shall be easier," Arabella suggested.

"Oh good idea." Bella tugged out a drawer and squealed, dropping it to the floor and barely missing Sophia's foot.

"Careful!" Sophia scolded, then glanced at the contents of the drawer. "Oh goodness."

Merry lifted one of the little boxes and peered at it. It was some kind of beetle mounted and pinned then put into a glass box. She shook her head and eyed the rest of the pile. There had been talk that her great-grandfather had been quite a collector and most certainly a hoarder. She had assumed that most of his collections had been dispersed upon his death but apparently not.

"I will never understand why men like collecting insects." Bella shuddered. "Horrible creatures."

"I imagine there are more in here. Perhaps we should leave the drawers where they are for the moment." Eyeing the dresser, Merry gave it another lift. "I think we can manage. There are four of us after all."

Bella wiped her hands down her gown as though the beetle had been crawling all over her. "The sooner we get that thing out of here, the better." She came to the side of the dresser and gripped it. Between the three of them, they were able to lift it easily.

Arabella hastened over to the door and held it open. "I should probably direct."

Merry nodded. "We will not be able to fit all four of us down the stairs like this anyway."

With a few grunts and a curse from Bella that they all ignored, they maneuvered the piece of furniture out into the hallway and to the top of the stairs. Pausing to suck in a breath, Merry folded her arms and studied the dresser then glanced at the stairs. This would not be easy.

"Perhaps I should go down backwards," suggested Sophia. "I am stronger than all of you."

"Older does not equal stronger," pointed out Bella.

Sophia straightened and lifted her chin. "Well, I am a good inch taller than you. And if the dresser falls, I have lived a long healthy, life." She thrust out her tongue.

Arabella giggled. Merry pressed her lips together. "You are four and twenty, Sophia. That is hardly ancient. Besides, I would rather you did not have to cushion any kind of blow." Merry tried to push the dresser to one side so that it did not block the stairs, but it was too large and angled oddly. "Perhaps we should just leave this somewhere..."

Bella shook her head. "No, we have come this far. We can manage, I'm certain. "You and I will hold onto the end while Sophia takes the weight. The two of us are strong enough to ensure it does not run over Sophia."

Merry blew out a breath. They could not leave it abandoned here. "Very well. Let us go slowly, though."

Between them, they inched it around. She and Bella took one end while Sophia positioned herself at the other, going backwards down the stairs.

"Be careful not to fall, Sophia," Arabella warned.

They managed to tilt the dresser and take the weight of it. Sophia gave a grunt, bracing herself against the end. Step by step, they slid it down until they were about halfway from the bottom.

"We're nearly there!" Bella exclaimed.

The weight of the dresser slipped a little. "Ugh, it's crushing me," Sophia complained.

Merry gripped it tighter to take the weight but it slipped again. "Something's wrong." It felt as though the dresser was being pulled down by something.

"I cannot hold it." Bella grappled to keep hold of her corner. "Sophia, move!"

Sophia jumped to one side as the dresser slipped from their grasp. A ripping sound followed the thud of the piece of furniture and the carpet on the stairs tore out from underneath Merry and Bella's feet.

"*Oof*!" Merry fell hard onto her bottom and Bella landed a step down from her. The dresser careened down the last few steps and Sophia let out a cry of pain as it swept past her. Merry suspected the furniture had run over her friend's toes. The piece of furniture came to a crunching stop against the front door frame, splintering the wood surround and sending the drawers shooting out.

Arabella dashed down the stairs, careful to avoid the torn carpet. "Goodness, are you well?"

"A little bruised, but fine, I think." Bella eased herself up and rubbed her bottom.

Merry stood and winced. She'd have a time sitting down for a while she suspected. "Sophia? Did you survive?"

Sophia plucked off a shoe. "I think so, but my shoe did not." She waved the delicate slipper at them. "And I shall not be doing any long walks anytime soon."

"I think we should get you sat down, Sophia," Arabella said. "You might have a broken toe."

"I think not." Sophia put her slipper back on. "The same cannot be said for the dresser."

"Or for my bottom!" declared Bella as she gingerly made her way down the stairs. "I think—" She snapped her mouth shut when two figures stepped into the open doorway.

Harry paused at the sight of all of them hobbling about and the broken dresser occupying the doorway. He took off his hat and a brow rose as he took in each of them.

Lord Thornford's lips quirked. "Having fun, ladies?"

Merry straightened her skirts and took in the mess of clutter at their feet. The drawers had been filled with more insects and rocks and shells by the looks of it. They had succeeded in making more mess than there was before.

"We were just..." Merry waved a hand. "Well, we tried to...you see..." She let her shoulders sag. "We had a bit of an accident."

Harry leaned against the doorframe. His lips were curved with amusement and creases surrounded his eyes. He was dressed to perfection, as usual, and she could not help notice how well he filled his waistcoat and remember how firm those arms were when wrapped about her. She forced her gaze down to the mess before he noticed.

"Do you think you might like some help after all, Merry?"

Behind her, she could tell her friends were nodding frantically without even looking at them. She pushed her shoulders back and with all the elegancy she could muster, she nodded. "Yes, I think that would be acceptable."

Harry's smile expanded.

Chapter Seven

A little rain broke the summer heat they'd been experiencing, bringing with it a beautiful rainbow that arched across the village, reaching down to the sands of Lulworth Cove. The scent of salt from the sea was strong today as a fresh breeze brought it across the cliffs. Harcourt did not take the time to admire any of it, however. He had more important things to do.

Griff was keeping himself busy, having already been invited to visit with several of the prominent families. Harcourt grinned to himself. He should have known the man would land on his feet with ease no matter where he went. At least it meant Harcourt could get time alone with Merry.

He strode up toward the Whitely estate. Hopefully Merry had not begun work without him. If yesterday was anything to go by, the woman would get herself into a pile of mischief and it would be up to him to dig her out. As much as he did not mind coming to her rescue, he was not certain Merry's pride could take another fall. She had the ability to grow even more defensive when hurt, like a creature striking out after injury to ensure its survival. Her cold father had never helped matters, he suspected.

He paused on the road to the dower house when he spotted a figure. And it was certainly not Merry nor her friends. He scowled. A man scampered around the building and stopped by one of the windows. Harcourt eased himself out of the man's view but was able to see him as he pressed his nose to the window. He could hardly be a thief, not with his elegant if slightly unfashionable dress.

Waiting, Harcourt watched as the man seemed to startle and scamper away. Though tempted to follow the stranger as he headed off down an ill-trodden path that would take him out onto the fields then to the main road, he did not much like the idea of leaving Merry unaccompanied.

What if the man was not alone? And what the devil was he spying on her for? It was no secret now that Merry intended to take over the dower house, particularly now that she was in conversation with the blacksmith and carpenter to help fix the building. Many were gossiping at how strange it was that a young woman should wish to lock herself away like that. Whoever that person was, he must have been looking for Merry.

The front door of the house was ajar. He shook his head. Anyone could walk in and accost her. Yes, they lived in a small, safe village, but that did not mean she should be blasé about her safety. There were no servants present today nor her friends by the sounds of it. He was certain if they were here, he'd know about it. He sighed. If that man had meant her harm, it would not have been difficult to get to her.

Pushing open the door, he paused abruptly. Glass shards were scattered across the hard-tiled floor of the hallway so that any visitor would tread almost immediately on them. Was this the work of that man? Had he been hoping to hurt Merry...or a visitor perhaps? And why? He jerked his head up at the sound of footfalls on the stairs.

"Stop!" he ordered.

Merry froze halfway down the stairs. Except for her startled expression, she was perfection. He was looking forward to her coming out of mourning wear but even in black, she made his heart race. There was something so damned enchanting about that forever befuddled expression and the way her crazed curls refused to be confined by pins.

He clamped his hands to his sides while he considered plucking those pins from her hair and thrusting his fingers into those soft locks.

"What is it?" she hissed. "Rolly?"

Frowning, Harcourt shook his head. "Rolly?"

"Yes, Rolly. The rat. Is he back?"

He chuckled. "No, Rolly is not back. Really, Merry, who names a rat?"

"Bella." She took another step down and he strode forward, glass crunching under his boots.

"There's broken glass everywhere," he explained, holding a hand out to her. "Your shoes shall never survive it."

"My shoes are quite sturdy."

He glanced down at the boots that peeked out from under her hem. They were no dancing slippers but nor were they as strong as his boots. "I am not taking the chance. Take my hand."

She scowled but put her hand in his and stepped down onto the bottom stair. Harcourt swiftly slipped a hand under her legs and swept her up into his arms.

"Oh!" Merry instinctively wrapped her arms about his neck.

Her gentle weight was expected. The need twisting about his insides not quite so much. Yes, he'd desired Merry for quite some time, but he'd always managed to keep it under control—except after the funeral. He could not help but recall how soft her lips had been and how perfectly she'd fitted against him. Just like she did now.

Carrying her into one of the drawing rooms, he set her down on a sheet-covered chair. "Stay here," he commanded.

Her eyes were still wide and her lips slightly parted when he left her to clean up the glass but at least he knew she'd stay in one place.

He made swift work of sweeping up the glass with a broom he found in one of the rooms then disposing of it. Satisfied with a job well done, he headed back into the drawing room to find Merry where he'd left her.

"Well, this is a miracle. Merry Bradford actually did what I told her."

The slight air of confusion snapped away and she stood. "There was no need for you to...to lift me. I could have stepped across it."

"And have glass embedded in your foot, I don't think so. Did you see what happened?"

She shook her head. "I have been upstairs in the bedroom for most of the morning." A smile curved her lips and lit her eyes. "I've made quite a lot of progress. It should look quite pleasant once I am finished."

"So you don't know how that glass came to be there?"

She waved a hand. "I probably knocked something over earlier. There's so much clutter and, well, you know what I'm like when I have my mind set to something. I was quite determined to get this bedroom clean."

He glanced over her dusty appearance. "I can see that."

And he knew well how Merry could be once she was occupied. The chances were she could have knocked over a glass of some kind and not noticed, but he doubted it. The presence of that strange man and the glass was too much of a coincidence, but why would someone want to harm Merry? He could not fathom a reason.

Harcourt shrugged off his jacket and laid it over the back of a chair before starting on waistcoat buttons. Merry eyed him, her lashes fluttering rapidly. He grinned. "Well, now that the glass is gone, why do you not show me what is to be done?"

"To be done?" Her gaze lingered on his arms as he rolled up his shirt sleeves.

"Upstairs?"

"Oh. Yes. Um..." She blinked and finally lifted her gaze to his. "There are some furnishings I need to rearrange, and I discovered more boxes of shells. I must find a home for them elsewhere. You could, um, make yourself useful doing that."

"Excellent. Feel free to put me to use anyway you see fit."

The rosy stain in her cheeks darkened.

"Are we alone today?" he asked.

"Yes." The word came out husky. "Yes." She straightened. "And if my brother were here, you know he would not allow it."

"Well, what Dan does not know will not hurt him."

At least he hoped not. Given Harcourt's past, he could not guarantee Dan would be thrilled about his feelings for Merry but once he proved he had good intentions, he could not see how her brother could complain. After all, he and Dan had been the best of friends since their Oxford days. Dan had to know Harcourt would never hurt Merry.

"Let us make a start then, before we are discovered." He winked, and she looked away from him.

The bedroom did not look much better than the rest of the house, but the windows gleamed, as did the armoire. Open boxes of shells and various stones were stacked up in one corner.

"I found them once we moved the dresser," she explained. "I'm not sure which of my ancestors loved shells so much but I suspect these are not the only boxes of them." She put her hands on her hips. "Goodness knows what I will do with them. It seems a shame to just discard them."

"I wonder if you might be able to donate some."

She picked up a small one and showed him. "They're hardly unusual. I could likely find another hundred on the beach if I tried hard enough."

"Perhaps we should have a sort through and find the best ones," he suggested. "But for now, I shall get these moved out of here. Where are you putting everything?"

"At the moment, I'm squeezing them into that bedroom." She pointed down the hallway to the room that had been cluttered with furniture and all sorts when he'd first visited.

Merry did not seem to comprehend how big a task she had ahead of her. Far be it for him to tell her, though. As far as he was concerned, she deserved better than being tucked away in a dower house, but at least it afforded him the opportunity to get her alone, away from the gossips and prying eyes.

Harcourt set to work clearing the boxes and stacking them in the other room while Merry stripped down the bed and swept the floors, sending clouds of dust everywhere. She eased open a window to let fresh air circulate.

Once she'd finished sweeping, she began lifting the paintings from the wall. Harcourt shifted the final box and helped her remove a particularly large painting and set it on the floor. Light had stained the ugly yellowed wallpaper, leaving dark marks where the pictures had once been.

"I shall have to find new wallpaper—and different paintings too." She nodded toward the one they had just removed which depicted a gruesome medieval battle.

"Charming. Just what one wishes to see before drifting off to sleep."

"Precisely. Whoever slept in here had strange taste. Though I am wondering if my great-grandmother or grandfather were quite strange in general. So many belongings and collections..." She shook her head. "I cannot fathom wanting to own so much."

"Well, perhaps a few years alone here and you shall follow in their footsteps," he teased.

Merry shook her head defiantly. "I like things tidy, as you well know. I cannot stand clutter."

"Yes, I know." His throat felt tight from all the dust so tugged at his cravat, drawing it lose and stuffing it into his breeches pocket. "Sometimes, I think I know you better than I know myself, Merry."

"Do not be silly." The words were a whisper. Her gaze was glued to the opening of his shirt.

A silent thrill of triumph ran through him. He was done skirting around this. Today would be the day he confronted Merry about her feelings for him and settled things once and for all.

Chapter Eight

After several more hours of moving boxes, cleaning, and re-arranging furniture, the bedroom was almost ready to be inhabited. Merry paused to admire their work. "A little paint and some wallpaper, and it should look quite charming."

Harcourt came to stand beside her. "If you say so."

"I do not know why people find it so strange that I might wish to live here."

"Because," he gestured out of the window, "you have a clean, spacious, modern home that anyone would envy over there."

"But it is not my home," she reminded him. "It is Daniel's now. I will simply be a lodger."

"This is technically Daniel's, too."

That was true. But she could not help feel if she put in all the work to clean it and make it livable again, then in some way, it would be hers. She would have poured herself just a little bit into the building.

"Daniel and Isabel need their space," she insisted.

"And you need yours." His lips quirked and Merry was reminded of how attractive those lips were, even when he was teasing her.

"To be able to work on my translation in peace will be wonderful," she said, turning her gaze forcefully away from him.

As helpful as he had been, lifting things she could not, Harry had been a distraction. She watched his muscles pull against his shirt and admire the slightly tanned flesh at the *v* of his shirt. She never quite understood how he managed to be tanned there as she rarely saw him without a cravat, but she suspected he must ride in a state of undress at times. Just the mere thought of him on horseback, his cravat discarded, sent a trickle of awareness through her that was entirely unwanted.

But quite pleasant, a voice whispered.

She forced the voice back. If her friends knew what she was thinking, they would be so upset. After all, *she* had been the one to suggest the forming of the Spinster Club. How could she give into desire for the opposite sex when her friends had suffered so terribly at the hands of men? Not to mention how foolish she would look once Harry turned his interests to another woman. He would have little intention of hurting her or ruining their friendship, but he was a man, and men were want to do such things.

"I could do with a drink," she declared, aware of the raspy quality of her voice. "All the dust is making my throat dry."

She did not look at him to see if he believed her. It was a plausible explanation anyway. Merry headed down one set of stairs and another into the kitchen that was set into the cellar. The windows at the very tops of the walls were grimy and covered in overgrowth outside the house, but that was something that would need to be dealt with later. For now, she lit two oil lamps and retrieved the lemonade and biscuits she had brought with her.

The kitchen looked as though it had been abandoned while someone was cooking a meal. Pots and pans remained on the stoves. Several bowls sat on various surfaces while cutlery was scattered across the table in the center of the room along with bowls, jelly molds, and a rolling pin. Although the room was dark and a mess, it would hopefully prove to be one of the easiest rooms to sort out. It needed no maintenance—just a good clean and tidy.

"Shall we take these upstairs?" he suggested. "It's a darn sight more pleasant than down here."

Merry smiled ruefully. "You have stepped foot into the drawing room, have you not?"

He nodded. "I shall admit peeling wallpaper and an inch of dust is not *de rigueur* but it has to be better than eating in the dark."

She had to admit he had a point. As she went to pick up the jug of lemonade, Harry reached for it. Their fingers brushed, and she jerked her hand back, holding it close. He smiled, a knowing look in his eyes.

She huffed out a breath. Damn the man. He knew full well what she had felt—and perhaps he had felt it too. Why was he so insistent on torturing her like this? They were meant to be friends, for goodness sakes, but this charm attack he had embarked on was driving her to the edge of her wits.

He said nothing when he picked up the plate of biscuits and carried them upstairs. Merry snatched up the two glasses she had cleaned up recently and followed him meekly, feeling anything but. How was it a mere touch of a hand could have her unraveling and thinking all sorts of odd thoughts? She had

touched men's hands before—albeit they had usually been rel-
atives, or it had been with gloves on. She must have touched
Harry's hands before though. It was that wretched kiss. It had
changed everything.

It had changed her.

But it did not matter. Life had not changed. She still intended to remain a spinster and Harry would go off and do whatever it was that Harry did—charm another widow into bed, most
likely. She owed her friends that much. Nay, she owed it to herself. She would not be like Arabella—swayed into bed with a
man who could so easily steal her heart.

She sucked in a breath and sat opposite him on a worn
chaise while he poured the lemonade. Turning her gaze to the
brown, peeling wallpaper in one corner, she pressed her hands
between her knees. She should tell him to go home. To never
come back. That she did not need his help.

Except she had tried that before and it did not work. One
thing she knew well about Harry was that he was about as stubborn as she but in a much more charming way. Somehow whenever he dug his heels in, the person on the end of the stubbornness found themselves acquiescing with pleasure. She had never
learned such a skill, so she usually ended up arguing with said
person.

"So what are your plans for the rest of the house?" he asked,
taking a bite of the biscuit.

Merry eyed his even, white teeth for a moment and how his
lips closed around the morsel. Taking a large gulp of lemonade,
she let the cool tang work down her throat before answering. "I
plan to keep it modest. Most of the furnishings can be cleaned

and used and as you know there is no shortage of paintings and decorations—although I shall not be keeping any medieval torture scenes on my walls."

Harry chuckled.

"I think even the rugs and curtains can be saved with a good scrub," she continued. "I have a small amount of savings I can use to redecorate, though the estate will fund the repairs. I am hoping Daniel shall see that as a good use of funds—we cannot let part of the estate fall down after all and perhaps he and Isabel shall live in it once their children come of age."

"I am sure he trusts your judgement implicitly, Merry. You have never been one to follow foolish pursuits."

She made a face. "There will be many who say the translation is a waste of time."

"Why would that be?"

"Because it has already been done. Several times."

"But none by a woman."

"Precisely. And each translation is slightly different. Every person puts their own touch upon the story. I hope to put mine on it."

"Well, I am certain you will do a wonderful job. I'm quite looking forward to reading it."

Merry lifted a brow. "You? Read?"

He leaned back in the chair and shook his head with a grin. "You really do have me pegged for a dullard, do you not?"

"I know you read..."

"But I have never read Greek myths. Yes, that is true. But I should very much like to read what you've written, Merry. Get a glimpse inside that clever mind of yours."

She could feel a blush rising in her cheeks. She was no simpleton, but it was different hearing such a compliment from a man like Harry.

"Why are you blushing, Merry?"

Holding a breath, she willed the heat to reside, then she took several more gulps of lemonade.

His lips quirked. "Anyone would think I had called you the most beautiful woman in the world. I only state the obvious—you are a clever woman. That is not something you are unaware of."

She fought for a response that would end this line of conversation. She had nothing. "I'm not blushing."

"I must need glasses then."

"Perhaps you do."

"You always did blush easily." He put a finger to his lip. "I wonder if you would blush if I told you that not only are you clever, you are incredibly attractive."

"Do not be ridiculous!"

"Ah, see the blush has increased."

She slapped her hands over her cheeks. "Why do you always insist on riling me, Harry?"

"Because it is about time we stopped skirting around this."

A lump formed in her throat.

"Around what?"

He cocked his head. "Do not play the fool, Merry."

"I thought you came here to help me, not insult me."

Standing, he strode over and sat next to her on the chaise. His nearness made her skin prickle. "The very last thing I intend to do is insult you." His gaze searched hers and for the life of her she could not look away. "I know you feel this." He lifted a hand and swept the back of his fingers across her cheek.

"I—" Blast him, his proximity was making thinking straight impossible. Her heart thrust against her chest, reminding her of how dangerous this was.

"Will you deny that you liked kissing me?"

That kiss. She almost hoped he'd forgotten it. She had certainly tried. But now he'd said the words, she was flooded with memories of heat and touch. Of being so wrapped up and lost in him that she never wanted him to release her.

"Harry..."

"Merry, you must realize I want to repeat that kiss." He glanced down and took her hand in his, lifting her hand to his lips and brushing his mouth over her knuckles.

The gentle brush made her boneless, and entirely unable to tug away from him. She searched his gaze and peered at his lips. She looked for every inflection in his expression for some sign that he was teasing her but for once, his expression was entirely sincere.

"Do you deny that you wish to repeat it too?"

"It-it was just a kiss. A very pleasant one, yes, but..."

"No. No but. Kisses like that do not come around often, believe me."

The reminder that Harry had probably kissed hundreds of women and she was merely another in a long line of them had her tugging her hand away. "I do not know what you want from me, Harry, but—"

"I want you."

"Well, you cannot have me," she blurted out, a slightly hysterical laugh threatening to burst through the words.

His lips curved. "You forget just how determined I am."

"Harry, I am not a conquest! In fact, I thought we were friends."

His smile widened. "Yes, that is true. You are not a conquest. And you are probably one of my very few female friends. Which is one of the many reasons we should be together."

"Together?"

"Damn it, Merry, I am not trying to proposition you into some sordid affair. I want to be with you."

"But-but you're a rake. Why would you want me?"

"Because I love you."

Time seemed to still. She fought for a response, but the words kept echoing through her mind, drowning out any logical thought.

"You cannot possibly. You are a rake. It is well known. You never remain with one woman for long." A slightly hysterical laugh escaped her. "You must be fooling yourself."

"Merry—" He took her hand again.

Merry whipped her head toward the sound of fast footsteps, shifting quickly to create a space between her and Harry. Bella appeared in the doorway, her face flushed. "Merry, quick, you must come now."

Merry glanced between Harry and Bella. She shouldn't have wanted to hear whatever he was going to say, but she did. More fool her. How many other women had been swayed by Harry's honeyed words and teasing?

"Merry!" Bella prompted. "Come."

Merry stood. "What's happened?"

"Oh, it's too hard to explain. But Arabella needs you. She needs all of us. But you especially."

"Why do I not leave you to it?" Harry suggested. "I shall see you tomorrow, Merry." He set down the lemonade and stood.

Merry opened her mouth to protest but his smile made any words die on her lips. Why did he have to make her stomach tumble and tumble with the merest smile? "See you tomorrow," she murmured instead as he dipped his head to them both and left the room.

Pressing a hand to her stomach, Bella drew in a breath. "That man...the one who broke Arabella's heart..."

Merry's eyes widened. "Do not tell me he is returned?"

Bella shook her head vigorously. "No, worse in a way. His brother is coming home."

Merry could not recall Mr. Russel's brother. Both had lived in Lulworth until he had ventured off to America, leaving Arabella behind with promises to return to her. That had been years ago, and she'd been a mere sixteen. None of them had known the men that well and none of them wished to. The brother had vanished off their social scene after his brother left.

"How is that worse?" Merry asked.

"Well, if Russel returned, there might be a chance he would still marry her...at least in Arabella's mind the returning of the brother, though, that shall just be salt in the wounds."

Merry pressed two fingers to either side of her head. "Yes, either way, it will not be pleasant for her."

Bella held out a hand for Merry. "Come on, Merry. We need to go and comfort her."

Merry took Bella's hand and let her lead her outside before hooking her arm through hers.

"I rarely seem to see you without Easton these days," Bella mused.

"Nonsense." The word came out more defensive than she intended.

Bella shrugged. "It is true. I know you are friends, but I am certain you two never spent quite so much time together before. He has taken quite an interest in the house."

"Well, as my brother's closest friend, he feels some sort of obligation to me." Merry kept her gaze pointedly forward as they made their way along the path from the house. "He probably thinks I shall do myself some damage if I do it alone."

A snicker escaped Bella. "Given the damage we created the other day, he might be right. But you two did seem cozy. Are you certain, he does not—"

"He is like a brother to me really," Merry declared before Bella could go any further.

"A handsome brother," Bella put in. "A handsome, tall, rich, charming brother."

"Is he?" Merry said lightly. "I never really noticed."

Chapter Nine

Harcourt took the early ejection from the house as an opportunity to look around the perimeter of Merry's soon-to-be house. He could not get that man's suspicious behavior from his mind. Perhaps his time in busy London had made him paranoid—after all rarely anything of interest happened in Lulworth. It was too small, and everyone knew everyone. It would not hurt to make sure things were well, however.

He paced around the back of the building and paused at some marks in the ground. On a wetter day, someone had been standing by the window and footprints were now cast into the dried mud. The overgrown grass and foliage showed signs of being pushed down.

Harcourt strode over to the window that the path led to and frowned at the window frame. There were patches of paint missing on the bottom of the frame, as though someone had been using a tool to pry it open. He rubbed a hand across his face. It was obvious there were no riches in the house—even with the clutter that was in there, little of it had value. No thief in their right mind would want to rob such a rundown house, and it had stood empty for years. Why would someone decide to steal from it now? His gut itched, much like before he was about to lose a card game. Something was not right.

He'd always intended to come back the next day. And the next after that. And many more. If he had not been interrupted by Bella, he'd have laid things out straight for Merry. He was not here to seduce...though he did wish to sway her a little. He was here because he loved her. But there were other things to worry about now too. He needed to keep a close eye on her if there was some danger to her person. How would he live with himself if something happened to her? He'd have to remain even closer than he'd originally intended.

By the time he'd finished his lap of the house, Merry and Bella were long gone. He began the journey home toward Lulworth Castle. The name of his ancestral seat was deceptive—it had not been a castle for over one hundred years when the original building had been knocked down to make way for its current incarnation. He made good time, walking from the Whitely estate, along the road and onto his estate. The large park surrounding the castle was always filled with deer and he could see them scattered over the hills that reached past Lulworth Cove and beyond.

The two towers of the building dominated the landscape, capping off a squared mock castle. Harcourt picked up his pace once he neared the building, entering via the servant's entrance.

"Is Lord Thornford still abed?" he asked one of the maids.

"Yes, my lord. I think May just took him a morning meal."

Harcourt nodded with satisfaction. As much as he liked his friend's company, it was easier to deal with Merry alone.

Making his way upstairs, he headed to the study. Lined with books on every wall, the room reminded him of Merry. When she had been younger and visited with her brother, she'd enjoyed the study almost as much as the library. She claimed its smaller proportions made a perfect reading space. He could almost picture her curled up on the chair in the corner whilst he dealt with estate business at his desk.

But it was no estate business that he needed to be concerned with now. He sat and dabbed the quill into ink as he drew out a fresh sheet of paper. No, his primary concern was Merry. Or to be more exact, what someone wanted with Merry. With her father recently dead, it seemed no coincidence that someone was spying on her.

There could be debts attached to the estate, he supposed. Perhaps her father had done business with some nefarious people. Whatever it was, he would not let Merry get tangled up in it. He penned a quick letter to his lawyer in London, requesting information on Merry's father and his dealings, as well as expressing the need for some investigating. If someone out there was looking to harm or threaten Merry in some way, he wanted to know about it.

As he sealed the letter, the door to the study opened. He swung a glance at it, expecting it to be the butler or his valet, but a bonneted head popped around the doorway.

"There you are!" His mother eased open the door fully and stepped in. She still wore travelling clothes but looked as glamorous as ever. "Goodness, you do look a mess."

Harcourt arched a brow. "It's nice to see you too, Mother. I thought you were still in Bath. I had no notice of your return."

She waved a hand and came to perch on the edge of the desk. With chestnut hair only marginally streaked with gray and a persistent smile, it was hard to remember his mother was ageing. She prided herself on being the center of all things social and could be counted on to liven up even the dullest of balls.

He suspected her attitude to socializing had rubbed off on him years ago and could be to blame for decadent years in London. Or he was simply making an excuse for himself. But he felt no shame over that time. That had been one segment of his life—the period where he figured out what he wanted—and this next one was another. With any luck, it would see him married and settled—with one woman specifically.

"I probably beat my letter home. The roads were so dry that we made perfect timing. So rare for this country."

"If I'd have known, I would have made sure I was home."

She leaned forward and adjusted his cravat then scowled. "What have you been doing? There's dust in your hair. Goodness, actually, there's dust everywhere."

"I've been helping a friend," he said simply.

"By getting dusty? My dear, I am certain you forget your position at times. One does not need to get dirty to help one's friends."

"A little dust never killed anyone, Mother."

She slid off the desk and smoothed down her skirt. "I am certain that is not true. I'm willing to bet that dust has killed at least one person." She grinned, her eyes twinkling. "Now, go and get cleaned and changed. I am hosting an 'at home' this afternoon."

He eyed her. "You cannot have been home long."

"And I am itching to see everyone."

"How will they even know you've returned?"

"Oh, they shall know." His mother's smile turned mischievous. "I ensured that I took the carriage directly through the village. Everyone saw my return. All my friends shall know I am home before long. Besides, we have a guest do we not? Lord Langley. I have not seen him in some time."

"You always did like to make an entrance." Harcourt stood, letter in hand, and gave his mother a kiss on the cheek. "Though Lord Thornford is likely still abed. He cannot get used to country hours."

"Well, he had better. He was devilishly handsome if I recall. I am certain many shall want to invite him to their homes."

Harcourt masked a smile. If his mother started meddling in Griff's love life, he would definitely want to return to London sooner rather than later. "It is good to have you home."

"Yes, yes." She brushed dust from his shoulders. "Now go and change. There shall be many eligible ladies visiting, no doubt."

He frowned. "I've changed my mind. You should go back to Bath."

She laughed. "Do not be like that. You are past thirty, my dear."

"Only just," he grumbled.

"It is high time you married, and would it not be nice to marry a local girl? There are many lovely ones who are just ripe for marriage."

Harcourt considered this. He could only think of one, and Merry was probably not what his mother considered 'ripe for marriage', particularly considering Merry seemed to be committing herself to some sort of spinster lifestyle by moving into the dower house. There were a few young ladies in the village who were of good breeding and had all the manners and refinements that his mother would like but none of them had ever interested him. He preferred his women with a little more courage.

"I have too much to do, I'm afraid, Mother. You shall have to entertain these *ripe* girls alone."

"Oh, you are wicked. Do you not see that I am ageing? I need grandchildren, Harry, and quickly. Not to mention, it's your bloody duty."

He chuckled at his mother's foul language. As much as she was the epitome of a grand lady in Society, there was no covering her bold personality at home.

"I shall do my duty, I promise." And hopefully sooner than his mother expected. "But I will not attend any 'at homes'."

She gave a dramatic sigh. "Well, you cannot say I do not try."

"That I cannot. Enjoy your tea and cakes."

He chuckled to himself when his mother swept out of the room. She'd been in Bath for several months and although he'd rather hoped she'd stay there while he dealt with the...Merry situation...he did not dislike having her home.

Though, he had no plans to tell her about Merry yet. She would approve, even if she did not think Merry was exactly countess material. Of course, his mother had been wanting him married for years, ever since the early death of his father really. He suspected her preoccupation with his marriage was not just her doing her motherly duty. It gave her something to focus on instead of grieving for his father. He'd be quite glad when he no longer had to deal with his mother's rather unsubtle matchmaking skills.

Perhaps, if he was clever, he could turn her attention to Griff. His friend might not thank him, but it would leave him time to worry about the Merry situation alone. He grinned to himself. Poor Griff had little idea what he had let himself in for when he'd decided to accompany him here.

Chapter Ten

A brisk wind fluttered the ribbons of Merry's bonnet. It blew in off the sea, bringing with it the fresh scent of salt. Bella looped her arm through Merry's as they made their way along the beach, not far from where the sea was slowly retreating in waves tipped with white.

Bella glanced back at Arabella who walked alongside Sophia and leaned in. "She is still terribly melancholy."

Merry nodded. Arabella had never been the most gregarious of them, but she was never miserable either. The recent news had affected her badly. Somehow, they would have to cheer her up.

The four of them strode up toward the end of the cove, where huge rocks jutted up and marked the end of the crescent-shaped beach and offered shelter from the breeze. Merry settled on the sand and peered out at the ocean. Guilt jabbed at her. While she had been contemplating Harry's handsomeness and getting herself tangled into an odd twist of emotions, Arabella had been hurting from the news. She would have to rectify that somehow, and certainly avoid any more thinking of Harry's strong arms or how he looked with his cravat undone.

A laugh threatened to bubble from her and she clamped down on it. To think he had said he loved her. How preposterous. He was either mad or teasing her. Whatever game he was playing, she was not falling for it.

Merry eyed Arabella, who had been wearing this odd strained smile for days. Already pale, her skin had taken on an ashen cast and it was clear she had not been sleeping.

"Stop looking at me like that, Merry." Arabella shook her head. "I know what you are thinking."

"I'm concerned for you, we all are," Merry said.

Bella nodded. "You have not been the same since you heard that snake's brother is returning to Lulworth."

Arabella's throat worked. "It is hardly his fault that his brother is a cad."

Sophia snorted. "He's more than a cad. He took advantage of you. He promised you marriage, knowing full well he would never return from America, he—"

A shiver visibly wracked Arabella. Merry put a hand to Sophia's arm. Out of all of the injuries her friends had suffered at the hands of men, Arabella's was the worst in many ways. The man who had stolen her innocence had sworn he would return for her once he had made his fortune, but he never did. No word ever came and Arabella was left waiting for many years.

And given her young age of sixteen, it had been a rude awakening to the folly and arrogance of men. Arabella was only lucky that no one had discovered her ruination, or she might have been sent off to Ireland or some godforsaken place like Miss Lucy Gable had.

"He is coming to look after his sick mother," Arabella said softly. "I cannot begrudge him that."

Bella frowned. "I do not remember the brother, do you, Merry?"

Shaking her head, Merry sifted grains of sand through her fingers. "He is older than us and he studied away for most of the time I believe."

Sophia nodded. "I believe so. And Mrs. Bryce said he has been in Scotland for some time and fears he will be all rough manners now."

"Well, wherever he has been, I will treat him courteously. He has done me no wrong." Arabella lifted her chin but Merry could not miss the slight quiver of her lips.

The brother might be completely innocent and for all they knew, could be a good man, but the family connection was still a sore reminder of what Arabella had given up to a man who had lied to her and used her in the most horrible way.

"I think we should all ignore him," determined Sophia. "After all, he shall be caring for his mother. I doubt he will have time to socialize with the people of Lulworth. We can pass him by quite easily should we see him."

"And if we do, we shall all be there for you, Arabella." Merry reached over and gave her hand a squeeze.

Arabella smiled. "I know you will. How I would have survived these years without you all, I do not know."

Bella waved a hand. "Oh stop, you shall make me cry."

"You never cry," declared Sophia.

Bella shrugged. "Maybe this will be a first."

Merry studied her friend. "It's true. I only just realized it. I have never seen you cry!"

"Well, you are not much of a crier either, Merry," Bella pointed out.

Merry shook her head. "You are worse I am certain."

"I think I am physically incapable. I must have no tears in me." Bella chuckled. "It's all that growing up with too many men. It's made me hard and unlovable."

"Nonsense. We love you. Well, most of the time." Sophia grinned.

Bella glanced around. "Come on, there is no one here. Let us dip our feet in the sea."

"It will be freezing," warned Arabella.

"I'm not scared of a little cold." Bella stood and slipped off her shoes, hanging them from two fingers. "Who is coming with me?"

Merry sighed and stood with a smile. "I suppose we have little choice."

The rest of her friends followed suit and they traipsed across the shingled sand until they reached the sea. Merry dipped a toe in and sucked in a breath. Despite it being the height of summer, the water was freezing, but that was always the way here. No matter how warm the days were, the water never warmed, and only the bravest of people swam in it.

"I never took you for a coward, Merry," Bella teased.

"I fear I shall lose my toes to the cold should I venture further."

Bella glanced around to check they were still alone and hitched her skirts up, taking a quick run into the sea until it was covering her ankles. Merry heard a muttered curse float in on the wind.

Behind her, Arabella giggled. Merry smiled to herself. Arabella's situation reminded her of how important their friendship and their newly created Spinsters Club was. Merry had been lucky to suffer little heartbreak in her life, and while her father had not been the best of men, Daniel had shown her what a good man could be.

Not that Merry wanted a good man of her own, of course. But her other friends all knew well of the foolishness and cruelty of men. Bella still suffered at the hands of her vile father and brothers—not that she ever, ever revealed the pain it caused—and Sophia still suffered from the memory of her marriage, Merry was certain of that.

They all waded in up to where Bella was. Cold bit at Merry's toes and she grimaced. "Why did we let you talk us into this?" she demanded of Bella.

"Because you know I have the best ideas," Bella declared proudly.

"Oh really? So that time when you stole our father's brandy and we drank it all until we were sick and could not move was one of your best ideas was it?" challenged Sophia.

Arabella clapped hands to her cheeks. "Oh yes, my head was sore for days."

Bella lifted her chin. "We had fun doing it, did we not?"

Merry chuckled. They had indeed had some fun times, especially when Bella decided to lead the way. She usually came up with the most scandalous and silly things for them to do and they never failed to have a good time together.

"I cannot feel my toes." Sophia waded back toward the beach. "I think that's enough sea for me."

"Me too," agreed Arabella.

Merry followed them both, leaving Bella in the sea.

"You are all spoilsports," Bella shouted to them.

Merry slipped on her shoes and folded her arms. "If you lose your toes to the cold, do not expect me to come and rescue you."

"Some friend you are." Bella stuck out her tongue and traipsed back to the sand.

Making their way back over to the spot by the rocks, the four of them sat. Merry plucked up a seashell and admired it. "Of course, now that I am in the dower house, I probably have hundreds of seashells just like this."

"What will you do with all the things your ancestors collected?" asked Arabella as she plucked off her bonnet and tidied her hair.

Merry lifted a shoulder. "I have no idea. It seems a shame to dispose of these collections that someone worked so hard on, but some of the things are utterly valueless and pointless. I mean, they did not even collect the best or the prettiest seashells."

"Perhaps you can find a few worth keeping then get rid of the rest," Sophia suggested.

Merry nodded. "I think I might have to. Harry suggested as much."

"I imagine it helps that you have Harcourt to help you." Bella's eyes twinkled. "I must say you two looked quite cozy, drinking lemonade in the drawing room like an old, married couple."

Instant heat filled Merry's cheeks. She glanced at Sophia and Arabella. Why did Bella have to bring up Harry now? The last thing Arabella needed was to think there was some romantic attachment between them. Which there was not. And there never would be.

"We were taking a quick rest." Merry jutted her nose up. "He had been helping me move things all day."

"He wasn't wearing his cravat or his jacket. I do not think I've ever seen him cravatless. He really is quite handsome."

Merry peered out over the sea. "Is he? I never noticed."

"She said that the other day." Bella rolled her eyes. "I do not believe her."

"You must be blind, Merry," Sophia said. "He is one of the most handsome men around here."

Merry looked at Sophia. "He has been friends with Daniel for a long time. It is hard to think of him as anything other than...a...a brother."

Bella giggled. "A handsome brother. A handsome, gentlemanly brother. How lucky you are to have him help you. I swear he is a much better man than most."

"He is a rake," pointed out Merry.

"He *was* a rake," Arabella corrected. Everyone peered at her. "What? I do listen to gossip occasionally. Mama says he is practically reformed, and that he has not taken any...lovers for some time."

Sophia nodded. "It's true, and you know Mama is never wrong in her gossip."

Merry drew in a breath. She preferred not to think of Harry's lovers. She'd known for some time—since she'd been old enough to understand really—that women adored Harry and he liked them too. But he never liked the same one more than once. His string of liaisons was as long as her bonnet ribbon. simply because Sophia and Arabella's mother said he was changed, did not mean anything.

Did it?

"Once a rake, always a rake," Merry declared, unsure if she was announcing it to her friends or herself. "We must guard ourselves, ladies. Despite all we know to be true about men, we are still too trusting. Remember our vows."

And she would remember them too. Especially next time she was around Harry.

Chapter Eleven

Harcourt smiled to himself. He'd know those wild black curls anywhere, even when tucked under a bonnet that was trying to escape in the breeze that whipped through the village today. Being on the coast of England was pleasant most of the time but it did mean being exposed to the wrath of the weather sometimes. He imagined Merry did not much appreciate it at present.

"That's the one with the dower house, is it not?" asked Griff.

"It is indeed."

"Too pretty to turn into a spinster already."

Harcourt clenched his jaw. "Stay away from her, Griff, she's far too good for you."

His friend lifted a brow. "I shouldn't worry. Your mother shall have me married and siring an heir within the month."

Chuckling, Harcourt paused by the old fountain. "That would make both of us."

"But you're not interested in being attached to just any woman, are you, Easton?" Harcourt swung a look at his friend who laughed. "I am not blind. Your preference for the spinster girl is obvious."

Harcourt watched Merry turn to speak to someone in the shop—the carpenter he assumed, given she had stepped out of his workshop—then made her way down the slope of the road in his direction. The wind lifted her bonnet and she was too late to grab it. He heard a soft curse come from her that made his grin expand. The errant headwear flew from her head, straight toward him. Harcourt made a grab for it and snatched it by its flailing ribbons.

She hastened over, and he handed it to her.

"Thank you," she said breathlessly, crushing it on top of those crazed curls. She tied the ribbon beneath her chin. "I wish this wind would leave us be. It has been like this for days."

He rather liked the wind—or at least the effect it had on Merry. It put color in her cheeks and a sparkle in her eyes, not to mention it sent strands of hair shimmering down her neck, touching it softly like a lover would. His fingers tingled at the very idea. Instead, he reached out and tightened the ribbon beneath her chin. Her pupils dilated. A tiny flourish of triumph lit inside him. He was a patient man and was willing to be endlessly patient when it came to Merry, but these tiny moments served to seal his determination. Whatever it was preventing Merry from seeing how amazing they could be together, he'd defeat it.

"Are you enjoying your stay here, my lord?" she asked Griff.

"I am indeed. It is quite refreshing to be away from London, and there is a lot more to entertain than I realized." Griff's gaze lit upon something behind Merry and he tipped his hat. "If you will excuse me, I see someone I must speak with."

Merry's gaze tracked Griff as he went over to speak to a group of ladies. Her expression soured. "He shall end up scandalizing one of them."

"Griff is a handful, but my mother is doing a marvelous job of keeping him occupied. Seems she thinks a bride from Lulworth would be perfect for him."

"I doubt a man like that has any desire to marry."

"You would be surprised. We men have been known to change our minds when the right woman comes along."

"I haven't seen you for a few days," she said, the color in her cheeks deepening.

"Did you miss me?"

"No!" Her eyes widened. "I mean..." She frowned and twirled a finger in the bonnet ribbon.

He chuckled. "So you did?"

"I was just wondering what you had been doing, that is all."

"My mother has kept my occupied."

"I'm surprised she has returned at the height of summer."

"She seems to think I need her."

"It must be nice to have her home, but I am certain she knows you can look after yourself."

"One would think so, yes, but I think she has another purpose for coming home. It is not just Griff she is determined to see wed."

"Oh."

There. He'd seen it even as she'd tried to disguise it. That little flash of hurt.

"Do you not think I should wed, Merry? After all, I am getting on."

"You are hardly ancient." Her throat bobbed. "But I suppose it is your duty, after all."

Though tempted to tease her further, Harcourt could not bring himself to. "What were you doing at the carpenters?"

"The rear door of the house is broken. I cannot fathom how. It seemed quite secure yesterday."

He scowled and straightened. The footprints he'd seen the other day and how it looked as though one of the windows had been tampered with combined with a broken door had him on alert. Something strange was afoot.

"Are you going back to the house now?" he asked.

Merry nodded. "I'm trying to clear the kitchen now."

"And you'll be there alone? Your friends are not helping?"

"They have done quite enough already. I only intend to do some light work for now."

"I shall come with you," he insisted.

"Really, there is no need. If I need your assistance, I will ask, I promise."

He lifted a brow. "Really?"

"I will," she vowed.

He rather doubted it. The stubborn woman had let him help once but he was certain she'd keep on trying to do it alone until she broke another piece of furniture and did some harm to herself. He could not let that happen and an uneasy sensation had settled into his gut about her being at the house alone. It was probably one of the few moments in her life she was alone. At Whitely she was surrounded by servants and if she was not accompanied by her friends, she was usually with her lady's maid.

"I'll come and help anyway. I have little else to do."

She narrowed her gaze at him. "I do not believe that. You must have estate business to see to."

He did, but it could wait a few more hours. If he had to work into the evening, so be it. More time with Merry and ensuring she was protected made a late night completely worth it.

"You underestimate me, Merry. I am supremely efficient."

She rolled her eyes. "And supremely arrogant."

He grinned. "Naturally."

"What of Lord Thornford?"

Harcourt peered in the direction of his friend who was surrounded by a gaggle of women and enjoying himself far too much. "I think he is otherwise occupied. I doubt he shall even notice I am gone."

They made their way back to the house, following the road up out of the village and onto her brother's land. Sunlight flecked between the leaves while the wind rustled the trees.

"I am glad I caught you, Merry. I thought we might be able to continue our conversation that was interrupted the other day." He paused. "I hope Arabella is well."

Merry's smile was slightly forced. "She is well."

"Good. In that case, I thought I might reiterate—"

"See?" she interrupted hastily. "The door is in dire need of replacement."

Harcourt inspected the door that had splintered on one edge. To him, it looked as though someone had kicked it in.

"Is anything missing?"

Merry shrugged. "I would say no but there is so much in the house, it is hard to say. Most of it is not valuable though, not even the paintings. I'm certain it must have been the wind."

He considered the exposed rear of the house. There were trees at the front, hiding it from the main house but the back of it was exposed to the weather. The recent wind could have blown it open, but he doubted it. He had no wish to scare Merry so he made a non-committal noise.

She was here alone. While he did not mind the opportunity to be with her, he didn't like the thought of it if it meant someone could have easy access to her. Whoever this someone was and whatever it was they wanted with her. Harcourt was going to have to spend even more time with her whether she wanted him around or not.

"Where shall we start?" he asked, already loosening his cravat.

Merry folded her arms across her chest. "I suppose I have no choice but to let you help."

"You could try to dissuade me, but you'd fail."

"I do not know why you call me stubborn all the time when it is clearly you who is the stubborn one."

"Perhaps, Merry, we simply match in stubbornness." He grinned.

She huffed. "A recipe for disaster."

"I disagree."

Her throat bobbed a little and she turned away to clear her throat. "Come on then. If I cannot get rid of you, I might as well put you to good use."

"I can think of nothing better." He drawled the words, ensuring she heard the hidden meaning behind them.

She ignored him and marched to the kitchen stairs. He chuckled to himself as her stomping footsteps echoed through the empty house. Merry put up a good fight but he could read her too well. She was struggling to fight this.

He joined her down in the kitchen. Several lamps and candles were lit, suffusing the gloomy space with a warm glow. The jelly molds and bowls on the table had already been washed and set aside to dry, and some of the side tables looked clearer. Harcourt drew off his jacket and pulled the cufflinks from his sleeves and tucked them in his pocket. Rolling up his sleeves, he clapped his hands.

"What would you have me do?"

She glanced at his bare forearms. Many men would not have noticed but Harcourt did. He saw her tongue dart briefly over her lips and her gaze linger before she lifted her eyes.

"Um, what if I wash and you put away?"

"Sounds good."

Merry set to work scrubbing the dust and grime off the various cooking implements while he stacked them away on the shelves and in cupboards. It took a good hour to get most it done and while he was no stranger to hard labor when needs be, he was glad he did not have to do such a laborious task every day.

"Now I know why cook complains when the kitchen is messy."

Merry laughed. "Me too. I shall never dismiss his words again." She lifted a jelly mold. "Who knew one needed so many molds?"

"I suspect one does not." He took it from her and their fingers brushed. The instant shock of sensation should have been something he was getting used to by now, but he wasn't. And nor was she. She tugged her hand away quickly and immersed it back in the water. "It looks as though your family liked to collect kitchen implements too."

"I have yet to find anything that is just a collection of one. There was even a drawer of soaps upstairs. All new and unused so I shall have to donate them somewhere."

"No doubt the church can find somewhere useful to send them."

"I can see why this house was all but abandoned now. No one wanted to tackle such a mess."

Harcourt leaned against the counter and eyed her. "Are you regretting starting this now?"

She shook her head vigorously, sending curls bouncing against her cheeks. "I know this is best for Daniel. And for me."

"I know you think balls and at homes are a waste of time, Merry, but surely you do not want to become a spinster before your time?"

"I do not see why everyone thinks a woman alone is so strange. Why can one not be content with one's own company?"

"One can be utterly content with one's own company, but not at the expense of life."

"I know how to live." Creases appeared between her brows. "Life is not just about balls and *at homes*, you know?"

"Believe it or not, I do."

She gave an unladylike snort. "Harcourt Easton giving up balls and parties...now that is stranger than me wishing to gain some peace and quiet to study."

"Is it really that hard to believe that I have tired of it all?"

A pot in hand, she paused and met his gaze head on. "Truthfully. Yes. Do not forget that by the time I was fifteen, you were already well-established in Society. Stories of you and your...time in Town were infamous. I cannot see you giving up such an...adventurous life." She lifted her chin a little. "And nor do I care if you do."

"That's not true."

"It is," she protested. "You are my friend, Harry, and I would no more wish a stale, staid life on you than I would wish a life of balls and celebrations on me."

"Perhaps, though, your friend wants other things in life. We are all capable of change. Surely even your books tell you that?"

Merry lifted a shoulder. "I—"

A sudden bang from upstairs sent Harcourt's pulse racing. He grabbed Merry and shoved her up against an alcove, flattening her to the wall with his body. She made a strangled sound.

"*Shh.*" He pressed a finger to his lips and listened.

"It was probably something falling. Or the wind," she hissed.

He turned, aware of her heart beating a tattoo against his chest.

Her breasts were crushed to his chest, her hips aligned almost with his. Underneath his fingertips, her arms trembled. He very much doubted it was with fear.

She drew in a ragged breath. "Harry?" she whispered.

He let his gaze linger on her lips, then along the pale freckles dancing across her nose. Inwardly, he chided himself. If there was an intruder upstairs, lusting over Merry was not his best move.

"Harry, you are crushing me." She tried to wriggle out from underneath him which only made things worse. Heat stirred in his body.

There was another thud, and Merry froze. He held his breath and listened again. Nothing more. Only the thump of his heart and the drip of a tap. Perhaps it was the wind again. But all his instincts said otherwise. And they were rarely wrong.

Spending time in London, even the more refined parts of Town, had left him with a keen instinct for danger. There were always plenty of thieves and criminals hoping to take advantage of the busy streets and lack of enforcement. Perhaps the strange man, and the footsteps and the broken door were nothing, but his instincts screamed otherwise.

Merry flattened her hands against his chest and pushed.

"Damn it, keep still, Merry."

"Harry, I do not know what you think you are doing but it was just the wind. Or something. Certainly no reason for you to...to..." She drew in an audible breath. "To be so close to me," she finished with a hiss.

He drew back, albeit reluctantly. If anyone caught them like this, Merry would be utterly ruined and as much as that might work in his favor, he had little intention of forcing her hand.

"Stay here," he ordered. "I am going to find out what that was." She opened her mouth and he pointed a finger at her. "Stay here. I mean it."

Merry pressed her head back against the wall and rolled her eyes. "Fine. I shall stay here and hide from the wind. Goodness, Harry, I never expected you of all people to be so jittery."

"Can you blame me, when I have so fine a woman to protect?"

Her brows furrowed, and lips pouted. "I do not need protection from the wind."

"So you do not deny you are fine?"

"Well, no...I mean..." She sagged. "Just go and find out what that was. I shall stay here." She made a motion of crossing her chest. "I promise."

"Good."

Harcourt made his way gingerly upstairs. Nothing save from the slight rattle of wind and a clock ticking somewhere could be heard. He checked out each room, one-by-one until he spotted an open window. The one that he had seen footprints by the other day. His palms grew clammy. That could not be a coincidence. For some reason, someone was trying to get access to the house. Or to Merry.

He finished searching the house but could find no more sign of an intruder or anything untoward. As much as he wanted to protect Merry from being fearful, her safety was more important. He'd have to tell her what he'd seen.

When he returned to the kitchen, he found her still pressed against the wall. She jolted slightly then straightened as he stepped off the final stair. He caught her quick look of relief that was masked hastily. Folding her arms, she gave him a smug smile. "I take it there was no great danger?"

"No." He eyed her. "But you were worried for me, were you not?"

"Do not be ridiculous. Why should I worry about what mere wind might do to you?"

"Is it so hard to admit you care for me?"

"Not at all." She swept a hand down her skirt, straightening out a non-existent crease. "You are my brother's friend. Of course I care for you."

"And your friend, Merry. Do not forget that."

"Of course not."

"You will need to get the carpenter to fix the window in the rear dining room. The latch is broken."

She sighed. "Another thing to add to my lengthy list."

He grabbed his jacket and shoved his arms into it. "In the meantime, I do not want you in this house alone."

"It will be days before the carpenter can fix it," she protested. "I have too much to do. Who knows when Daniel will return."

"With these winds, a good while longer I suspect." He took her hand and led her upstairs, ignoring her little tugs on his arm. "I will not have you alone in an unsecure house."

"Harry, this protective, overbearing attitude is getting a little tiring." She wrenched her hand from his once they reached the hallway. "I know you feel an obligation to look after me, but I am a grown woman, and am completely capable."

"Do you not think I know that?" If he was in a less concerned mood, he'd probably be thinking exactly how grown up she now was. "But something is amiss. Someone is trying to gain access to the house."

She made a dismissive noise.

"Or to you," he added.

Merry opened her mouth, then shut it. Then opened it again. "Why would someone wish to get to me?"

He shrugged. "I cannot say, but it is not a risk I am willing to take."

Tilting her head, she eyed him. "Have you had an accident and not told anyone about it? A hit to the head perhaps?"

"Of course not."

"That would explain…" She waved a hand up and down. "All this."

"All this?"

"Why you think a spot of wind is an intruder and why you believe someone might wish to harm me. And, of course, why you…Well…" Her cheeks colored.

"Well?"

"Why you are talking of…why you keep…" She bit down on her lip and readjusted her glasses despite them being perfectly in position.

"Why I am talking of you and me, you mean? Of love?"

She swung her gaze to the clock in the hallway. "Oh, look at the time. I should be heading back to the house."

Harcourt chuckled. The clock didn't work and still read seven o'clock. "I shall walk you."

"There is really no need."

"I insist. I shall see you to the tree then you can walk alone from there. No need to be seen with a rake like me then." He grinned.

"I was not fearing for my reputation," she insisted. "I just do not need an escort. It is only a quick walk down the road and I am on my brother's land."

"I know that. But I am still accompanying you."

Merry gave a great huff. "See? Far more stubborn than I ever am."

"More determined too, Merry," he warned. "Far more determined."

Chapter Twelve

"But that is far more than we were paying before my father died!" Merry eyed the older man who had adopted a smug, sort of *I know everything look* as soon as she had stepped in the door.

"I am sorry, my lady, but that is just the way it is. For that many candles, I must charge you that much. You are welcome to buy from elsewhere..."

She narrowed her gaze at the candlemaker. He knew full well she would have to negotiate with someone in Brycesbury—the nearest town—if she did not buy from him, and the chances are the price would be no better. Whether they would treat her any better than Mr. Langford did, it was hard to say. The man clearly thought her incapable of running her brother's household and was taking advantage of the fact she had never done it before. Even so, she was not foolish.

"I fail to see why the cost of candles has increased by nearly twenty percent. Your materials are unchanged."

The dark-haired man gave a shrug. "It's business, my lady. It's hard to explain."

His patronizing tone made her breaths feel hot. For his age, Mr. Langford was an attractive man with short dark hair peppered with gray, a strong jaw, and clear blue eyes. His work kept him muscular too. She had never really had occasion to talk to him before now but as soon as she had stepped foot in the chandlery, he had tried to charm her. When he had realized that would not work, he had become condescending.

"Either the costs of your labor have increased within a month's time or the cost of your materials have. Or have you perhaps purchased new tools?"

His jaw tightened. "As I said, my lady, you are welcome to purchase from elsewhere."

Merry clenched the order for candles in her hand until the letter shook. The house needed hundreds upon hundreds of candles to remain lit. It was an extremely profitable order for Mr. Langford, and she knew he did not wish to lose it. But he also knew she had little choice. Tears burned behind her eyes and she blinked them rapidly away.

Spinning on her heel, she stomped out of the building. Fresh sea air struck her face, instantly cooling the heat in her cheeks and eyes.

She inhaled deeply. She must not cry, she must not cry.

Exhaustion made her bones ache and her mouth dry. Running a household the size of Whitely Grange was no mean feat.

Yes, she knew well enough how to plan meals and organize the servants, but it was the other things—like buying enough candles so they did not all have to sit in the dark. Not to mention the running of the estate land and handling problems with tenants. Her father had never anticipated she might have to fill her brother's shoes for a while and neither did she. She was making it up as she went, and it meant late nights after working at the dower house, and little sleep.

And far too much stress. Especially when arrogant men like Mr. Langford thought he could take advantage of her because of her sex.

Pressing fingers to either side of her temple, she drew in another breath but felt her chin quiver. Oh, if only Daniel would return home, or these winds would abate. No doubt the crossing would take twice as long with such choppy seas. If it was bad just in the cove, it would be awful out at sea.

"Is all well?"

She lifted her gaze and bit down on her lip. Of all the people to meet, it would have to be Harry. Just when she was at her weakest moment. He peered at her from under the brim of his hat, his eyes filled with concern. It made the tears well up again.

"Y-yes, all is well," she managed shakily.

A brow rose. "Is it?"

She sighed. "It's just that Mr. Langford is trying to charge me an exorbitant amount for candles. I know he has raised the prices because he is dealing with me."

"Indeed." He glanced at the slip of paper in her hand. "Is that the order?"

She nodded.

Harry snatched the paper off her before she could protest. "Won't be a moment," he said cheerfully, ducking into the doorway of the building.

Merry opened her mouth to protest but it was too late—he had vanished into the shop. She huffed and pressed her back against the whitewashed wall. This was not what she wanted. She was a strong woman. A woman who was meant to be learning to function alone. Without the help of men. But now Harry had swept in and taken over, and she was left standing around like a fool.

Several moments passed. Perhaps Mr. Langford would not acquiesce to Harry either. Merry was not sure if she would be pleased or not. She needed those candles, but not at that price. The estate could not afford such a rise in expenses, and she had no wish to appear as though she could not handle things while Daniel was gone. But at the same time, if Mr. Langford would not budge for Harry either, she would feel a little vindicated. Perhaps it was not about her sex after all.

Harry's expression when he left the building had her in no doubt that it was entirely to do with her sex.

He handed her back the order slip. "All arranged," he declared.

"At the original price?"

His lips quirked. "With a slight discount for inconveniencing you."

She stared at him, at his confident expression, then at the agreement that stated a discount. To her dismay, a sob bubbled out of her. Harry's expression quickly changed to concerned.

"Merry?"

She covered her mouth and turned away. Tears sprung from her eyes and dripped quickly down her cheeks. It was all too much.

How was she meant to achieve everything she wanted whilst doing a job she never thought she would do?

"Merry?" Harry put a hand to her shoulder, twisting her around to face him. "What on earth is the matter?"

"I cannot even find the time to work on my translation!" she blurted and tried to turn away.

She had no time, and no help. It was all so much harder than she expected. The estate manager was excellent but treated her much like Mr. Langford did, as though she were a child who had no brain in her head. How utterly lonely it was trying to run an estate on her own.

"Come." He glanced up the empty street and took her hand.

She had little willpower to resist. The morning had left her drained and boneless. Her eyes and lungs hurt from trying to hold back all the emotions simmering just below the surface. She let Harry lead her out of the village onto the hills that overlooked the sea.

The wind blew fiercely, and she pressed a hand to her bonnet, but the day was not cold. The sea covered the horizon, broken up only by a few fishing boats. Even with a heavy covering of cloud, the cove was beautiful. The semi-circle beach offered up almost white sand and the sea was known to be bluer here than many other places in England. Sometimes she forgot how wonderful Lulworth was and how lucky she was to have such beauty a mere walk away.

Harry released her hand. She could feel him watching her while she eyed the scenery and drew in calming breaths. Finally, she turned to face him. "I'm sorry."

"For what?"

"For..." she waved a hand back toward the village. "For that. For being so snippety."

"For crying? For being defensive? I do not think you have anything to apologize for, Merry. Mr. Langford was trying to take advantage of your situation."

"What did you say to him?"

"That I was not impressed with him taking advantage of a grieving young woman and that I would take Lulworth Castle's business elsewhere if he did not rectify the situation."

Merry gave a soft smile. It was still aggravating that Mr. Langford would only negotiate with Harry but, for the moment, she would take the reprieve. It was one less thing for her to worry about.

"Thank you."

"I am sorry you are having to deal with these things alone." He stepped close, touching a finger to her cheek. "If there is anything I can do..."

"I am sure you have enough work, looking after your own estate. I knew it kept my father busy, but I did not understand quite how much work was to be done. And I am certain I could manage it," she said hastily, "but I was never taught any of it. I am having to learn as I go."

"You always were a quick learner."

"Not quick enough. I fear the whole estate will have crumbled to pieces in the fleeting time Daniel has been away." She clamped her bottom lip under her teeth as another swell of emotion rose up within her.

He reached for her and she was powerless to resist. Harry drew her against his chest. He smelled of spice and soap, and he was warm, oh so warm. Muscular too. She knew all this, of course, but her mind would not let her forget that fact. In Harry's embrace, she had never felt so protected, so...so unalone. She closed her eyes and listened to the steady heartbeat as she pressed her cheek to his chest.

He rubbed a hand up and down her back in a soothing motion. All the anger and frustration fizzled away, leaving her relaxed but...well, slightly achy and hot. Once the emotion had died down, she became too aware of that muscle, too wrapped in the scent of him. She should pull away and yet she could not. Her limbs were utterly useless, rooting her in place.

He eased back and used a finger to lift her chin. His green gaze searched hers. A little wind riffled his hair and she found her gaze dropping to his lips. They looked soft and warm. From memory, they probably would be. Suddenly, it did not matter how windy or exposed it was, she was too damned hot. Somewhere inside her, a voice whispered. It warned her to flee. To tear from his arms. Unfortunately, that voice was overpowered by another. *Stay,* it told her. *Stay and kiss him.*

The loud voice triumphed. She remained in his arms and let him smooth a hand across her cheek.

"You have no idea how beautiful you are, do you, Merry?"

The words created something warm and fluffy inside her. Which was ridiculous. She had never much cared about her appearance. Her hair was too curly and hard to maintain and after a good bout of sun, her freckles grew too dark. No one had ever called her beautiful. If anything, she was...acceptable. Nothing more.

But, damn the man, the words took their intended effect. She almost felt beautiful as he eyed her, his gaze tracing what had to be every inch of her.

His other hand rested on her lower back, keeping her close.

"Every time you speak, every time you look at me, I feel as though I am powerless." His words were slightly husky. "All I can think of is how much I want to kiss you."

She could create no words. Her mind tried to wrap itself around Harry's confessions, but it could not. Instead, she gaped up at him, utterly lost to the magic of his voice and his body.

Harry tilted his head. Breath held, she waited. *He's going to kiss you, Merry.* She wanted to argue with that stupid voice. She knew very well he was going to kiss her. And God help her, she wanted to be kissed. It didn't matter that this was Harry—a rake of the highest regard—or that they were out in public and all it would take was someone to walk by to ruin her forever. Had she learned nothing from her friends?

Apparently not. She closed her eyes and absorbed the feel of his warm palm, then the brush of his breath over her lips. Behind her closed eyelids, Harry was just a man, a friend, a gentleman, and they were not out in public but somewhere secluded and safe.

His lips upon hers galvanized her. It was a sweet kiss for a mere moment, until the torrent took hold. When she latched her arms around his neck, he made a raw sound in his throat that sent thrills through her. The feeling of being beautiful remained. The sensation of being wanted and adored and capable of stirring such passion in this man made her feel powerful.

Stop, that quiet voice muttered somewhere. She searched for the louder voice, the one that urged her on and discovered that it had been her all along. Once Harry coaxed apart her lips with his own and brushed her tongue with his, the voices were gone, and it was only her and Harry.

Her and Harry and this delicious, delicious kiss. She was starting to understand all the epic love in Greek myths. If some of the characters kissed like this, no wonder they all did ridiculous things in the name of love.

Merry pushed her fingers into the hair at the nape of his neck and felt the softness of the strands. In response, he held her closer, forming her body to his. She fit him like oil pouring into a bottle, filling every curve and nook. She could not be quite sure where she started, and he ended anymore, only that it felt too right to be here, wrapped in his embrace and drinking in the taste of him.

A ripple of wind riffled her hair. It whispered to her, taking the place of her sensible inner voice. But she could not break away quite yet. She drew back slowly, loosening her hands from around his neck then letting him ease the kiss to a gentler one until he pressed one tender one upon her lips. Merry opened her eyes to find him staring down at her, his pupils dark.

"Merry, we should be together. You cannot deny you want me."

The words were a cold, stark shock, as though a wave had reached up from the sea and swept her away. Of course, she wanted him. Physically. But how could she have been so foolish to give the man an inch? The smug smile quirking on his lips made her push away from him.

He released her.

"You think this is a game?" Her hands shook, so she clenched them at her side. "Anyone could have seen us."

"I think we were both aware of that," he drawled. "And I do not think this is a game. If it is, I am losing sorely."

"How so? You can get away with kissing any woman you like at any moment. I, on the other hand, certainly cannot kiss a man without consequence."

Damn him, why did he have to look at her in that way? With that sort of wry amusement that warmed his eyes and sent them digging straight down into her soul. If she let those voices dictate to her again, she'd be back in his arms before long.

Remember your friends. Yes, remember them. Remember the pains they had been through at the expense of men. And she could not forget Harry's history. She never thought he'd be the sort of man to play games with a woman he purported to respect so she could only conclude that he was bored, and his mind had tricked him into thinking he had feelings for her. Perhaps he did have some, but they would be minor and fleeting.

Unlike hers. It would be all too easy to fall entirely for Harry, and where would that leave her when he tired of her?

Much like her friends—heartbroken and aggravated by the world of men.

"I am losing, Merry, because it is utter agony to be around you and not be allowed to touch you or kiss you. I am losing because you keep denying what is between us and what it could—what it would—become." He took off his hat and swept a hand through his hair. "I have cared for you for a long time, Merry. I should like to do that for the rest of my life too."

The words struck her hard in the chest. How easy it would be to believe that. To fall into his arms with promises of being cared for by him for the rest of her days. But it was all a lie, it had to be.

"You are lying to yourself, Harry. I could not keep you content for long. You are not a foolish man, you must know that."

"You are right. I am not a foolish man. I know myself and I know what I want." He put his hat back on. "What I want is you."

She folded her arms over her chest as if she could prevent the words beating into her heart. "You will see that you are wrong soon enough."

He shook his head. "No, you shall see that you are wrong, Merry. It is only a matter of time."

"You will be waiting an eternity I fear."

He shrugged. "You're worth the wait."

Oh lord, how was she meant to keep her defenses up against such words? She turned away and eyed the horizon, picturing her friends and their vows. She recalled Arabella's recent hurt. Even if she could survive such heartbreak, what sort of friend would she be if she turned on her vows to them? No, he could say all the honeyed words he wanted but she would not give in.

Harry came to her side, leaning in and making her skin prickle. "Are you going to the kite festival tomorrow?"

She frowned. Why had he gone from declarations of...well, something...to the kite festival?

"Um, yes."

"I shall see you there then." He eyed her for a moment. "Be careful, Merry. something strange has been going on at the house, I'm certain of it. I would not wish you to come to harm."

She shook her head. A bit of wind and a broken door did not add up to danger, not to her mind. Still, she turned to face him. "I will be cautious," she promised. Why she even owed him such a promise, she did not know.

"Good. I could not live with myself if anything happened to you."

She tightened her arms about herself. "Stop."

"Stop?"

"Stop with your words. Your-your nice words. I cannot stand them."

"I had no idea nice words were so offensive." Harry chuckled. "I shall see you tomorrow, Merry, but I cannot guarantee what sort of words I will use."

Merry avoided watching him as he left her on the hilltop. Tomorrow was the annual kite festival where all the villagers and some visitors from surrounding towns would bring their kites to the beach and fly them for everyone to see. It had always been something she looked forward to—it was the sort of socializing she quite enjoyed. There was no need for polite conversation or silly rules that she could never quite get her head around.

Now, however, she could not decide whether she was looking forward to it or dreading it.

You cannot wait to see Harry again. She rolled her eyes at herself. *That* voice needed to go.

Chapter Thirteen

"I can find nothing of note, my lord." The grizzled-faced fellow chewed on a lump of tobacco, swilling it about his mouth. The private investigator had a hard look in his dark eyes that told Harcourt he'd seen too much of life. Regardless of his appearance or tobacco habit, the investigator was one of the finest in the country, highly recommended by Harcourt's lawyer.

Harcourt nodded and pushed a hand through his hair. "You are certain?"

The man nodded. "Her father had no untoward dealings, no angry ex-lovers, and the brother is just as clean. This family has nothing to hide and no reason for anyone to harm them."

Harcourt let out the breath he'd been holding. So he was being paranoid. Perhaps the chap who'd been stalking around the house was merely curious. After all, the house had been empty for some time. He probably wanted to see what all the activity was about. And the broken door and open windows really had been due to the wind.

Merry was safe.

Standing, he offered the investigator his hand. "My lawyer shall see to your fee."

The investigator nodded. "Have a good day, my lord."

After the investigator left his study, Harcourt sank down onto the chair and rubbed a hand across his mouth. A smile curved his lips. Merry might not be in danger but it did not mean he was planning to ignore her now. Not after that kiss. Why she was so insistent on denying everything she felt, he did not know. He'd felt the damned thing all the way down to his toes. When she kissed, she poured herself into it, and had been as swept away as he had. Passion like that did not come along every day. He just needed to convince the stubborn woman as much.

"Has he gone?"

His mother thrust her head around the door to the study.

"Yes, Mother."

"Good." She stepped into the room and smoothed down her elegant gown of purple silk. Feathers bobbed in her hair. "He had a frightful look to him. I do not think you should spend time with such men."

"He was an investigator, Mother. There was nothing untoward about our meeting."

She did a loop of the room, running her finger along the fireplace then over the spines of several books. "Why do you need an investigator?"

"A business matter, that's all," he said vaguely. If there really was nothing to be concerned about with regards to Merry, he did not need his mother worrying too.

She came to a stop in front of him and ran her gaze over him. "Are you coming to the kite festival?"

"Of course. It would be rather remiss of the Earl of Langley to miss the most looked-forward to event in Lulworth."

Creases appeared between her brows and she perched on the desk in front of him and began tugging at his cravat. "Be sure to be nice to any ladies present."

"I am always nice," he drawled.

"Well, be extra nice." She tutted. "Your cravat is not straight."

"Don't tell my valet that."

"Men are never the best judge of these things. Even ones supposedly trained in the art of dressing gentlemen. I always think valets should be women. We have an eye for these things."

"I cannot image there are many women who would wish to earn their living dressing men."

His mother chuckled. "A handsome man like you? I should imagine you would have hundreds of women clamoring to dress you." She slid off the desk. "Just as there will be many looking to spend time with you today."

He managed not to roll his eyes. His mother had been trying to marry him off since the day he inherited the title. She meant well, but no man needed their mother thrusting women their way every second of the day.

"I shall try my best not to disappoint you, but do not expect a marriage proposal today, Mother."

"Does that mean there might be one in the future?"

He smiled. "I shall try my best."

She narrowed her gaze at him. "You are just saying that to appease me. I swear, I do not know what men have against marriage these days. It is getting harder and harder for women to gain a proposal. You are all too busy enjoying bachelorhood."

"You would rather I was married miserably then?" he teased.

"Of course not. You know what I mean. There are many lovely girls who would make excellent wives. You are not getting any younger, and neither am I for that matter."

"Ah, so this is all about your desire for grandchildren."

She sucked in a breath. "Well, of course it is, Harry! You need an heir, and fast." Her expression softened. "But I would so like to see you happy. Your father and I might not have had as much time together as I would have liked, but I will treasure the years we had together. I want the same for you."

"If you want the same for me, stop thrusting poor, unsuspecting women my way."

His mother huffed and lifted her chin. "I do not see what you have against the women I pick. They are all charming."

Charming, yes. Beautiful too, usually. Sweet, kind, and polite. All the traits one might want from a wife.

But none were like Merry. None had the fiery personality and the quick wit of her. No one would ever compare.

"How about this, Mother...let me worry about which women I wish to talk to today, and I promise I shall attend your next *at home* and be nothing but charming and lovely to whichever ladies attend."

She pursed her lips and eyed him. "I suppose that would be agreeable."

"Excellent. Do not forget you have Lord Thornford to find a wife for, too."

She grinned. "Yes, he is quite a catch. And far more amenable to my attempts." Poor Griff. Still he supposed Griff was at least enjoying all the attention. He couldn't quite fathom why his friend had yet to leave for London. Harcourt had hardly had a moment to spend with the man, but he was damned good at occupying himself and establishing a better social life than Harcourt had.

He offered his mother his arm. "Come then, Mother. I assume the carriage is ready."

She gave his cravat one last tug, then took his arm.

Griff joined them in the carriage. "So what is this kite festival all about?"

Harcourt shrugged. "It's been happening for as long as I can remember. I am certain there was some reason for it, but I have little idea why."

"I think it was something to do with one of the wars," his mother muttered. "We probably saw off invaders on the beach with kites or some such."

Griff's expression grew bemused. "What a quaint tradition."

"What of Miss Arabella Pemberton," Harcourt's mother declared. "She's a sweet thing with respectable parents. A little shy perhaps but there is nothing wrong with timidity. Far better to be shy than outrageous."

He should probably put his mother out of her misery and tell him that he'd already found the woman for him, but the last thing he needed was his mother forcing him upon Merry. His mother would scare her entirely and ruin any slight progress he had made.

"Outrageous like you, you mean?"

She gave a gasp. "I am certainly not outrageous."

"You are hardly prone to timidity," he said dryly.

"Just because one is not shy does not mean one is outrageous." She paused and waved a hand. "Anyway, I am an old widow. I can do what I wish. No one minds if an older woman is outrageous."

"Oh look, we're here."

"You do not need to sound so glad about it."

Harcourt chuckled and gave his mother a kiss on the cheek. "Have fun, Mother. Leave the courting to me."

She snorted. "If I leave it to you, there shall be no courting whatsoever."

"You promised."

She sighed. "Yes, I know."

Stepping out of the carriage, he handed his mother down and straightened his hat.

"Oh, there is Mrs. Georgeson." His mother unlatched her hand from his. "Be good," she warned.

Harcourt grinned. "I am always more than good."

With a tut, his mother left them. The kite festival had been happening in Lulworth Cove for as long as he could remember. He had never been sure why it had started but as the local nobility, he was always obliged to attend. In his younger years, he'd found it tiresome. There would be few women to entertain—none that he could truly enjoy the company of without expectations anyway—and most of his friends resided in London, even Daniel for the most part of the year.

Last years had been different, though. He could still recall Merry, the wind riffling her hair with a flush on her cheeks. Her laughter skittered across the sand, drawing his attention. It had not been the first time he'd noticed she had grown into an attractive woman, but it was one of the more prominent moments. One that had etched itself into his mind and built up until he could deny it no longer—his feelings for her had changed.

"Well, all the ladies are here." Griff grinned. "And quite a fine selection too."

"You're enjoying the countryside now then?"

"All these untouched, sweet country women. I can almost see why you were so keen to return home. Though I suspect only one woman was responsible for that."

Harcourt sought her out now, scanning the crowds of children and adults gathered on the beach. Kites already filled the sky—some rudimentary and made from little more than twigs and paper while there were other larger silk ones, filling the sky with color. Thankfully the day promised to be clear and sunny, but the breeze filled the cove as though lingering especially for the festival.

He took the time to walk amongst the kite-flyers, greeting many of the villagers and stopping to converse with the prominent businessmen of the area. He introduced Griff to a few of the people he had not met yet but most already knew of him, particularly the young women who all sent flirtatious looks his way. It was not often they had another titled man in their midst after all.

The whole time, however, he had a target in mind.

Merry stood on the outskirts of the group with her three friends. Her kite was at odds with her mourning wear—a bright purple and green diamond that she flew quite masterfully. He could not help stealing glances her way, admiring the color in her cheeks and her wide smile as she concentrated on keeping the kite aloft.

Griff leaned in. "Go on then. I can occupy myself. As I seem to be doing with increasing regularity."

"You invited yourself here," Harcourt pointed out. "You will not make me feel guilty."

As he neared Merry, she met his gaze. Her smile dropped as did the kite, swooping down. Harcourt ducked at the last minute, barely avoiding a collision with the kite. He picked it up from the sand and carried it over to her.

"If I did not know better, I would think you were aiming for me."

The color in her cheeks remained and darkened. She bit down on her bottom lip and took the kite from him. He had no doubt she was recalling the last time they were together. And if she was anything like him, she was thinking about whether there would be a repeat of the moment. Of course, Merry would be battling the instinct whereas he was more than happy to give in. If only he could teach her to let go of control a little.

"The wind caught it," she blurted out. "I had no control, I—"

"Miss Arabella, what a fine kite you have." He turned his attention to Arabella. "As do you all. I am grateful you did not try to take my head off too."

Arabella blushed. "I would never attempt such a thing, my lord."

From the corner of his eye, he saw Merry glower at him. He had to fight hard to mask a triumphant smile. For a woman who claimed she wanted nothing to do with him, she played the jealous lover well.

"Shall I help you fly them?" he asked the ladies.

Bella hoisted hers into the sky with the help of Sophia. "No need, my lord. I'm an excellent kite-flier."

He turned his attention back to Arabella. "Miss Arabella?"

"Oh, no. Please do not bother yourself. Sophia can help." She eased away.

"What are you doing?" hissed Merry.

"Offering my help, I believe."

"Arabella is shy, you know that."

"I do not think I did anything wrong, Merry. I was merely offering my help to a lady in need."

Creases appeared between her brows. "None of us are in need, Harry. We are quite capable."

"Humor me. Let me help you just once and I shall leave you to it."

Merry huffed. "Fine."

He stepped back and lifted it into the sky, letting the wind catch it. Then he hoisted it high and watched it soar upward before joining Merry again. She kept her focus on the kite—deliberately he was certain.

Coming to her side, he watched the kite while Merry directed it to swoop and soar in the sky. Her tense posture eased, and a smile curved across her lips when she brought it down low then lifted it high again.

"Have you been secretly practicing?" he asked.

Her smile expanded. "I am just an excellent kite-flier."

"Hmm, I do not recall you being quite so talented last year."

"Just because I am better than you." She flicked a teasing look his way that made him want to tear her away from the event and kiss that cheeky smile into submission.

"No one is better than me."

She handed over the strings. "Very well then."

He took the strings and a sudden gust caused the kite to drop to the ground.

She giggled. "Oh yes, I see now. No one is better than you, my lord."

"You sabotaged me," he protested. "Get it flying again and I shall show you who is best."

Merry stomped across the sand and lifted the kite again, thrusting it up with all her might. The wind blew again, forcing the kite sideways and downwards. The strings wrapped about Merry and she stilled, effectively trapped.

Harcourt laughed as he made his way over to her. She huffed. "I cannot decide if you did that on purpose."

"I certainly did not. Now stay still." He began to unwind her, but she moved, and he gave the strings a tug, tightening them about her arms.

"You're making it worse!" she exclaimed.

"You are making it worse. Keep still or you shall be forever at my mercy."

She froze at this threat, her lips a mutinous pout. Harcourt continued untangling her, lifting the strings up over her head and allowing the backs of his fingers to brush her neck. He met her gaze and saw her pupils widen.

"Got yourself in a tangle there, Easton?" Griff strode over, grinning.

Harry leaned in and murmured, "This is not over, Merry."

Merry's cheeks filled with color. Harcourt wanted to say more but Griff's vicinity prevented him from doing much other than releasing her from the kite.

A lone figure up on the hillside caught his attention and he stilled. He stared at him until realization dawned. It was hard to tell but it looked an awful lot like the man who had been snooping around the house.

He thrust the kite back into Merry's hands. "Excuse me, I just need to do something." He strode off toward the path that led up to the hill. He was going to find out once and for all what the stranger wanted.

Chapter Fourteen

Merry gnawed her bottom lip as she made her way down the slope of the road away from Arabella's house. If only there was more she could do. The news of the return of this brother still shook Arabella. Merry kicked a stone from the road. If she got her hands on the man who had ruined her...

Lord, sometimes these men so aggravated her. As much as Arabella tried to insist she was well and had forgotten about him, it was clear it still haunted her to this day. She had waited for so long for him to return for her, clinging to hope. Merry could hardly imagine what that must have been like, anticipating every letter and having her heart broken over and over when the man never came back. As a friend, she felt so powerless against the past. If only there was more she could do.

She trudged along the road, hardly noticing her surroundings. What if there was some way they could cheer her up? She'd have to talk to Bella and Sophia. Their usual walks on the beach and tea together would not suffice, but Arabella was not one for visiting the bigger towns or spending time with lots of people. Nor were the rest of them particularly, but Arabella's shy disposition meant she loathed big gatherings the most.

Perhaps—

The pounding of hooves and the rattle of wheels drew her attention. A shout came from behind her and she spun. A blur of horses and a carriage were upon her before she had realized what had happened. Jumping back from the road, she sucked in a breath. The conveyance whipped by her, sending a cloud of dust up around her. She closed her eyes against it and something hard struck her shoulder. Pain exploded through her body and she was knocked backward, sending her tumbling to the ground.

Peeling open her eyes when she came to a stop, she eased herself up on both palms, wincing when a sharp stab of pain tore through her shoulder. Her palms were raw too and her body felt bruised. She lifted her head to eye the carriage vanishing around a corner. The driver had neither stopped nor slowed to check on her.

"Jesus Christ, Merry." Large hands were upon her, lifting her to her feet before she could connect the voice to the person.

Harry gripped her by the elbows, his face etched with concern.

Merry blinked and drew in breaths, her head slightly fuzzy while her pulse pounded through her. Any closer and that carriage could have...

"I saw what happened. The bloody idiot could have killed you."

She nodded slowly, unable to summon a response through a dry mouth. She glanced at her shoulder and winced. Blood tinged the torn sleeve of her gown. He really could have killed her. She was lucky to be alive.

Harry scooped her up, his arms a warm cocoon around her. She felt utterly boneless and entirely at his will. His muscles were firm and reassuring against her palm. He carried her over to a fallen tree and set her down. Were it not for his arms about her, she might have collapsed onto it anyway.

It was only then that she realized Lord Thornford was with him. The man leaned over her. "Is she alive?"

Her thoughts were still slow, and her limbs felt warm and loose. She forced herself to keep taking long, deep breaths but the fuzzy sensation would not quite leave her.

"Yes, she's alive," he snapped at his friend. Harry sat down beside her and rubbed a hand up and down her back. "Lean forward," he ordered. "Take deep breaths."

She did as she was told and kept breathing until some sense of normalcy returned. And annoyance. What sort of fool driver went at such speeds along these country roads?

"I did not see him coming," she finally managed to whisper.

"I know. He was coming too fast," Harry agreed.

"And I was not concentrating."

"You should not have needed to. This was his fault, Merry. I swear, if I find out who did this..."

Lord Thornford let out a sound of disgust. "The man was an idiot. I have never seen such reckless driving. It was like he wanted to hit you."

She shook her head. "I cannot imagine it was anyone local. They would know better."

Harry peered at her shoulder. "May I?"

She peeked up at Lord Thornford who took a few steps back and turned away. She was unable to see the full extent of the damage, so she nodded. It stung but she did not think there was any permanent damage. Her body might tell her otherwise to-morrow when she was stiff and bruised from the ordeal.

Drawing out a handkerchief, Harry lifted away the torn fabric.

"I have a habit of ruining your handkerchiefs. I still have your other one up my sleeve if you want to use it."

Out of the corner of her eye, she saw him grin. Blast, she should not have admitted that. She could not help it, though. He'd given it to her at her most vulnerable moment and there was something horribly soothing about having it upon her person.

"I'm glad you kept it."

"Well, I could hardly waste a fine handkerchief, could I?" She grimaced when he dabbed at the wound. "What are you doing here anyway?"

"I was coming to see you at the dower house. To see if my help was needed." He pressed the napkin against her shoulder. "And to talk to you."

"Harry—"

"I think you are in danger."

A laugh escaped her. "In danger? Why would I—"

"Think on it, Merry. There have been too many coincidences. Broken glass, broken doors, windows forced open. and now this."

"This was an accident!" She glanced at him, taking in his furrowed brow. "Harry, you cannot be serious."

"I'm deadly serious. I did not tell you this, but I saw a stranger lurking around the dower house not long ago. I did not wish to frighten you, but I saw him again yesterday, watching you."

She frowned. "Watching me?"

"At the kite event. I tried to follow him but had no luck. Even you must admit, you have had a run of bad luck recently."

"The door was simply the wind. As was the window. I do not know why some stranger might wish to watch me, but you cannot think that all adds up to danger."

"I certainly can." He drew the handkerchief away from her arm. "No permanent damage I think. Just give it a clean when you get home."

"Think logically," she insisted. "Why would someone wish to harm me? I am of no threat to anyone."

He shrugged. "I only know what I've seen. And even you with your logical mind, you must admit a great many strange things have happened."

She made a scoffing sound. "You think someone might be trying to kill me? By way of breaking doors and forcing open windows?"

"All I am asking is that you be careful, Merry. Do not go anywhere alone. Not until we know for certain that no one is trying to harm you."

She folded her arms and regretted it when her hurt shoulder pulled. Instead, she put her hands into her lap. "I am not sure how you intend to ascertain that, especially when you do not know who this stranger is and can come up with no logical reason why someone might wish me harm." She held up a hand. "I will admit, there has been a few strange occurrences at the house, but none of those add up to someone wanting to hurt me. This incident" —she motioned to the road—"was a horrible one, but hardly intentional. Who could have known I would be walking along here alone at this time of day?"

"I did. I saw Arabella in the village and she said you had visited. Many people would have seen as much, especially if they had been following you."

"The only person following me, is you." She jabbed a finger into his chest.

"And thank goodness I did or else you might still be lying on the ground."

She sucked in a breath. The concern in his gaze was real and she had to admit, this accident had rattled her. But she was not some wealthy, powerful woman with secrets and suchlike. No one could have any reason to want anything from her. What did Harry expect from her? That she might spend the rest of her days being escorted about just in case his strange conclusion came true?

Lord Thornfield cleared his throat from behind them. "Are we all decent?"

"Yes," she said weakly.

He strode over to the log and glanced her over. Merry tried not to fidget under his appraisal. She did not know Harry's friend that well yet, but he seemed to be making himself popular with everyone in Lulworth. With dashing good looks and a flirtatious manner, it was easy to see why, but she preferred to avoid flirtatious manners and extremely good-looking men.

Not that she managed to avoid Harry at all.

"What should we do with her?" Lord Thornford asked Harry. "I could carry her home if you wish."

"Over my dead body," Harry said tightly.

Lord Thornford shrugged. "I am stronger—that is why I suggested it."

Harry scowled. "Like hell you are. I've bested you at boxing many a time."

"Um—" Merry started.

"Boxing has nothing to do with strength. You are lighter, so you are quicker on your feet," Lord Thornford declared.

Harry stood and Merry swung her gaze between the two men as they faced off against one another. The light-headedness had almost vanished now and aside from a stinging pain in her shoulder, she felt almost recovered. No doubt her shoulder would be stiff and bruised tomorrow but there was no chance she was letting either of these men carry her.

"I am simply lighter on my feet, *and* stronger." Harry folded his arms across his chest. "Besides, Merry hardly knows you. *I* am an old family friend. If anyone is to do the carrying, it is me."

"Were you not complaining of a sore back the other day? I am only trying to do you a service." Lord Thornford huffed. "Apparently this is what I get for trying to be a good friend." He looked to Merry. "Who do you want to carry you? This oaf...or me." He flashed a grin.

Merry opened her mouth to reply but the words were stuck. The idea of either man carrying her was implausible. If anyone spotted her in the arms of one of them, she would be ruined, and she was not at all sure she would survive a journey huddled up against Harry.

"See?" Lord Thornford motioned to her. "She wants me to carry her but does not wish to offend you. You have put her in an awkward position, Easton."

"Actually"—Merry stood—"I do not need to be carried by either of you. I think I shall manage the walk by myself." She began walking down the road at a careful pace, waiting to pick up speed until she knew for certain her head was clear.

Harry and Lord Thornford hastened to catch up with her. "Let us at least escort you home. I do not wish you to be alone," Harry said.

"Because Easton has this crazed idea you are in danger," Lord Thornford said. "Best to let him do what he needs to do," he confided with a grin.

"So you think it is preposterous too?" she asked Lord Thornford.

Lord Thornford leaned in. "If I were you, I would let him play hero. It makes life a lot easier if you just go along with whatever Easton wants."

Harry gave a grunt. "You two make me sound as though I need carting off to the lunatic asylum."

Merry sighed. "Very well, you two can escort me, but as soon as we are in sight of the house, I wish to be left alone. You know how Mrs. Kemp feels about gentlemen visitors."

"Bloody Mrs. Kemp, whoever she is." Lord Thornford exclaimed.

Harry chuckled. "I feel exactly the same."

Peering between both men, Merry held back another sigh. How on earth did she keep getting herself into these situations?

Chapter Fifteen

Harcourt stilled at a knocking sound coming from the dower house. He doubted Merry had heeded his warning yesterday—or realized quite how terrified he'd been when he saw that carriage strike her. She'd been so damned close to being killed that he hadn't slept a wink all night.

Something that had not passed Griff, his mother or his estate manager's notice. He had dark circles under his eyes as proof and he couldn't prevent himself from yawning. If anything would have happened to her...

If anything did happen to her...

He found the front door of the dower house open and followed the sound of hammering. If someone else didn't kill Merry, he'd have a tough time not throttling her himself. Fool woman was determined to be careless with her safety. Why did she think leaving the door open, so anyone could walk in, was acceptable?

"Merry?"

The hammering noise stopped, and a head peered around the corner of one door. "Lord Langley. Whatever are you doing here?"

"Mr. Nicholson. I was about to ask you the same."

The carpenter stepped out from behind the doorframe and lowered his hammer. "I was fixing this window. Seems it took a battering from the wind. Then I'm to finish up the door. Lady Merry left for Brycesbury after issuing her orders not long ago." The slight smile on the old man's face had Harcourt imagining Merry had been quite specific in her orders.

"I do not suppose you know why she was going to town?"

He pressed fingers to his forehead. "Said something about wallpaper." He shrugged. "I try not to listen to ladies' conversations, but I think that was what they said."

"They?"

"Miss Sophia Pemberton?"

Harcourt nodded. Sophia might not be the sort of escort he had in mind for her, but it was better than no one he supposed. Still, it was clear she had not taken him seriously. He'd have to remedy that.

"Thanks, Frank. Have a good afternoon."

"And you, my lord."

The hammering resumed as soon as Harcourt left the building. He had not planned on going to Brycesbury today, but he could do with speaking to his accountant anyway. If he so happened to find Merry while he was there, so much the better. He could reassure himself she was well, and he'd be damned if the woman didn't need another speaking to. He pushed a hand through his hair and put his hat back on. He'd always known Merry was a handful, but the bloody woman was turning him gray. If she was not kissing him as though he were the only man in the world then refusing him, she was determined to put herself in danger.

He made his way back to Lulworth Castle and found Griff stepping out of the doorway.

"Chasing after a certain woman again?" his friend asked with a grin.

Harcourt ignored the question. "I'm heading to Brycesbury. Do you want to accompany me?"

"Why not? I could do with a stretch of my legs."

"I'm riding in. It's a little way on foot." Harcourt led the way to the stables where they fetched horses. Thankfully several were already saddled, ready for exercise so he did not have to waste any time waiting. Brycesbury was only a forty-five-minute brisk ride away so he'd have a good chance of meeting Merry there. He'd have to ready himself for her ire at being followed but he did not much care at this point. So long as she was safe, that was all that mattered.

Pushing his horse as fast as she could muster, they made it to Brycesbury in even quicker time. The town was smaller compared to the likes of London or even other towns in Dorset, but it was the nearest to Lulworth and boasted many shops. For those who did not wish to travel far, it was ideal. His mother complained there were no fashionable people or interesting places in the bustling town, hence her frequent trips to Bath, but he rather liked the quaint air of the place.

He grimaced. Now he really did sound old. Merry was having a strange effect on him. Was it not enough that she had persuaded him into the idea of matrimony without even trying? Now he was comparing Brycesbury to London—and favorably so.

"An attractive place," Griff commented, "but what are we doing here?"

"I need to see my accountant." Harcourt dismounted and tethered the horse to a hitching post. "Do you want to explore the town on your own while I visit with him?"

Griff shrugged. "I am well-used to being abandoned by you these days."

"Need I keep reminding you that you invited yourself here."

His friend held up a hand. "Yes, yes, I know. I am an utterly unwanted guest. It's a fine job this neglect is in pursuit of a woman or I would be sore about it indeed."

"You're not unwanted, Griff, but you did manage to choose the worst time to decide you like the country."

"I will confess, there is something diverting about it."

Harcourt chuckled. "You mean there is something diverting about all the ladies that you have never met before."

"The country air does seem to breed attractive women," Griff mused. He glanced around. "I see a coffee shop. Leave me there and I shall meet you in an hour."

Harcourt nodded. "That works."

Leaving Griff, he set off toward the curtain shop, ignoring his accountant's place of work entirely. He would worry about that once he had assured himself Merry was safe. He found the shop to be empty once he arrived and the shopkeeper informed him that two young ladies had been in a mere ten minutes ago. Harcourt must have just missed them. He thanked the shop-keeper and headed out once more, scanning the streets for them.

The town was not as crowded as London but nor was it de-signed to house as many visitors as it did. The streets were narrow, only allowing for a single carriage to pass and stalls were set up on street corners, forcing pedestrians onto the busy road. He stopped by a stall selling hot crumpets and scanned the crossroads. There were plenty of women in bonnets and pretty gowns, but his gaze landed upon two women—one in color and the other in black.

He picked up the pace and hastened after them as they entered a small park through iron gates. He saw Merry talking animatedly to Sophia without any care for her surroundings.

Scowling, he moved into a quick stride. Damn the woman. She should be paying more attention. While she and her friend strolled along the pathway between two lawns, Harcourt could see a man following behind them, his clothes ragged and his manner suspicious. The man paused briefly to see if there was anyone else in the park.

Harcourt started to run but the busy paths made it hard to catch up with Merry and he knocked into several people and was nearly struck by a carriage. He pushed past a large man, muttering a quick apology, his gaze set on the man following Merry.

His heart lifted up into his throat as the man approached. He grabbed Merry's arm and she turned. The sunlight caught a glint of something. His blood ran cold.

A knife.

Shoving through a couple strolling arm in arm, he raced toward the park, turning the corner and shoving through the iron gates. "You there!" he bellowed.

The man twisted, his eyes widening under a floppy hat, then pushed past Merry. He raced down the path and darted in between the trees. Harry hurried up to the women and grabbed Merry's arm.

"Are you well?" He sucked in a breath. "Did he hurt you?"

"I-I-I am well." Her skin was ashen.

He looked to the trees. No doubt whoever he was knew the town better than Harcourt and would be long gone.

"And you, Miss Sophia?" he asked.

She straightened. "I am fine. He seemed more interested in Merry." She wrapped an arm around Merry's shoulders. "Goodness, I never thought we would be victim of a robbery in a town like this."

"Was that what he wanted?" demanded Harcourt. "To rob you."

Merry shook her head. "He never said. He just pulled out his knife then ran off as soon as he heard you shouting."

Harcourt's heart stilled. This right after the near carriage accident. This was no coincidence. "Did you get a good look at him? Was he scrawny?"

"I suppose." Merry glanced at Sophia.

"I was too busy looking at the knife," Sophia confessed.

"Old?" he asked.

Sophia shrugged. "A little old I suppose. Dark hair."

Then it was not the same person who had been at the dower house. But he did not think the carriage driver had been either. Whatever this was, there was more than one person involved in trying to harm Merry. Somehow, he was going to have to discover what the devil was going on—and fast.

"I think we should get you home," he said to Merry and Sophia. "You look pale, Merry."

She nodded slowly. "Yes, that might be an idea."

"Lord Thornford is in town with me. We shall escort you both home."

Merry shook her head. "Oh no, there is really no need. We can—"

"I will not accept a no," he said firmly. "We are seeing you home safely."

For the second time that week too. Whoever was trying to hurt her was becoming more determined and bolder. If he was going to keep Merry safe, he would have to take action. Next time something happened, he would be close by and he certainly would not let the bastard get away.

Chapter Sixteen

Merry paused to study the drawing room. With the chairs clean and in place, the windows gleaming, a few choice ornaments scattered about the room, it almost looked livable. It was a shame about the rest of the house, though. There was still much to be done.

"Where would you like me to start, my lady?" asked the maid Merry had managed to steal away from the house.

"If you start over there." She motioned to the windowsill. "And I shall start with the fireplace, then we shall see if we can tackle the chandelier together." Merry looked up at the crystal chandelier. It was not as grand as the ones in Whitely Grange or Lulworth Castle, but it would still take some cleaning and they'd have to stand on the table to do it.

Brandishing a cloth, Merry dampened it in a bowl of water and set to work cleaning the dust and grime from the top of the fireplace, working her way down to the cornicing. The methodical, repetitive movements were somewhat soothing—allowing her to drift into a world of thoughtlessness. That was until the maid knocked into a vase, making it rattle on its table.

Merry whirled, heart pounding. A hand to her chest, she drew in a breath. "You startled me."

The maid grimaced. "Forgive me, my lady. I know you are still jumpy."

Sucking in a breath, Merry smiled. "It's fine. I am fine."

The news of the attack had spread quickly—most likely thanks to Bella who had heard all about it from Sophia. It had been three days since it had occurred, and she had been fine since. Nothing had happened. Nothing would happen. It was just one of those things...

She frowned. One of those strange things. She still had no idea why a man should pull a knife on her, nor why all these other things had happened. As much as she hated to admit it, Harcourt might be right. What if someone did wish to hurt her?

She straightened and set back to work. Even if there really was someone trying to harm her—and she could not fathom a reason why—she would not let them dictate her life. She had already taken to ensuring she was never alone and Harcourt had inserted himself into her life more than ever. There had not been a single day since that she had not seen him. Glancing at the clock on the mantelpiece, she gave the face a thorough scrub and scowled. He would have normally checked on her by now. Where was he today?

Blast, was she really anticipating his arrival? Looking forward to it even?

She shook her head at herself. It really would not. Yet...yet she could not help herself. She missed his smile, the way his eyes creased at the corners when he looked at her, the deep timbre of his voice.

Lord, she even missed the way he made her feel—how he tangled her up inside until she did not know which way was up or which was down. She had not seen him for all of an evening and a morning, and she missed him! It was ludicrous.

A crashing noise made her heart bound again and she flung down the cloth to face whatever it was that had caused such a noise. Fists lifted, she found herself confronted by a large, black and white, shaggy and awfully muddy dog. The creature bounded over to her, jumped up to give her a lick across the face, then sprung over to the maid. Emma squealed when the dog pressed its filthy paws to her apron before jumping onto a chair then off again.

"What on earth...?" Merry made a grab for him but he darted out of reach, knocking into a side table and sending a vase to the floor. Thankfully it landed on the rug, saving it from disaster. The same could not be said for the dog.

Its tongue lolling from its mouth, it darted out of the door. Merry heard a crash from down the hallway and glanced at Emma. "Where did he come from?"

The maid shrugged. "We need to get him out before he dirties everything!"

Merry noted the muddy prints and splatters everywhere. He had almost undone all their hard work. She snatched her skirts. "I had better see if I can stop him."

She followed the sound of chaos, dashing down the hallway and into the rear dining room. The dog did an excited loop of the room, forcing her to chase him around the table. "Come here, doggy," she cooed.

The dog paused and tilted his head but the sound of the carpenter working on the door must have caught his ear as he cocked his head and raced in the direction of the back of the house.

"Damn doggy," she muttered, taking off after him again.

A cry of annoyance came from the carpenter and Merry found the dog on top of the man, licking his face. "Get off me, damn dog." Mr. Nicholson fought to get the great animal off him.

"Here, doggy," she tried again. "Good, doggy. Why do we not find you something to eat?"

The animal paused at the word *eat* and lifted his head.

"That's right," she said softly. "Come with me. Let us find you some food." She backed away slowly, coaxing the dog to follow her.

He took a few steps, inching closer. Merry stopped and continued to motion with her hand. "Are you hungry" She glanced underneath him "...boy?"

Just as the dog was within grasping reach, he sprinted off again. Merry cursed under her breath. If this continued, the whole house would be in chaos. She gave chase once more, following him down into the kitchen which was almost all organized. At least it had been. The dog knocked its big body into one of the tables, sending jelly molds and copper bowls to the floor. The crashing sound startled the dog and he darted under the large table in the middle, his body quaking.

Merry shook her head and squatted to eye him. "Silly, doggy. You are not so bold after all, are you?" She stretched her hands out. "Come here and I shall give you a biscuit."

The dog inched out from his hiding space and gave her hand a lick. Apparently enjoying the taste of her, he gave her wrist a lick, then her forearm. She took the opportunity to grab him by the collar. He rewarded her with a long, wet lick across her face. Merry scratched behind his ears and rubbed his head.

"That's better, is it not? After a bath, I think you would be a fine dog, if a little clumsy. But I know about clumsiness."

"Ah, there you are."

Merry peered at the boots in front of her then followed them up and up until she met Harry's gaze. He grinned down at her. "I see you've met Orion."

"Orion?"

"Rather appropriate name for your dog, do you not think?"

Standing, she brushed her hands down her skirt. Orion had apparently appeased his need for chaos and stood dutifully by her side. Likely waiting for a biscuit, she concluded.

"My dog?"

He nodded. "He used to be a sheepdog for one of the farmers on the estate but he's getting a little old for the job now."

Merry smiled down at the animal. "He seems to have all the energy of a pup."

"And he is getting naughty in his old age." He leaned forward and gave the dog a pat on the head. "He's loyal, though, and could be good protection for you."

She opened her mouth then closed it. As much as she wanted to protest the preposterous idea that she needed protection, that niggling feeling would not leave her.

"You shall have to forgive his muddy state. He was perfectly clean when we left but somehow found the only mud puddle in existence at the moment."

She shook her head at the dog as he looked innocently up at her. "I do not think you deserve one, but I did promise." She plucked a biscuit off a plate on the table and gave it to him. "I'm sure he'd prefer meat but that's all I have."

Harry chuckled. "I think he will eat almost anything."

The dog lowered himself and munched happily on his reward then dropped his belly to the floor, resting his head on his paws.

"Is he really called Orion?" she asked.

He nodded. "Perfect for you, do you not think?"

She let her lips curve. She'd never had an animal. Her father had not allowed it, but she'd always thought she might get a cat one day—a peaceful creature that would curl up on her lap as she studied. But looking at Orion's now peaceful face as he regained his energy, she could picture him settled at her feet quite easily.

"You are being quite presumptuous, Harry."

He stepped close. "You need protection, and Orion here can look after you when I am not around. As much as I would like to be present at all times...I cannot be. Unless..."

Her mouth dried a little. She shouldn't ask it. She knew where this would lead. But she could not help herself. "Unless?"

"Unless something changes. Unless you give me a reason to be constantly at your side. As your friend, I can only spend so much time with you in the eyes of Society. But—"

Orion barked and lifted his head. Before Merry could grab him, he was off again, racing upstairs.

"Oh no." Merry grabbed her skirts and glanced at Harry "I thought sheepdogs were obedient!"

"They usually are. I think he's excited to have you as his owner." Harry grinned. "I cannot blame him."

Merry rolled her eyes, then gave chase. They followed the sound of barking out into the garden where Orion bounded around the expanse of grass like a madman. They watched him for several moments.

Harry chuckled. "I think he will like it here."

She nodded. "I think so too. He seems a good dog, if a little unruly."

"It's the new setting. He will calm down soon enough." He turned to look at her. "Keep him close, Merry. Then I will not have to worry about you so much."

"You do not need to worry for me, Harry."

"Even after the other day?" He drew off his hat and pushed a hand through his hair. "I think I aged a hundred years witnessing that."

She bit down on her lip. "It was very scary, but I am fine. I'm sure it was just...a coincidence."

He lifted a brow. "You still believe all of these things are co-incidences."

No. But how could she admit as much when she had spent the past weeks insisting otherwise? How could she admit she was scared and that she wanted to leap into his arms and have him wrap himself around her until she could forget anything and everything? Her friends would never forgive her, and she would never forgive herself.

"I am certain I will be fine. Daniel should be home any day now and things will return to normal."

Harry shook his head. "Is that what you wish? For things to be normal?"

She plastered on a smile. "Of course."

"I don't believe you."

"Harry..." She was interrupted by Orion coming to lie by her feet.

"It seems you are his mistress already." His eyes were warm and inviting.

She could feel it happening, the way her heart softened at the sight of the dog curled up beside her. And at the way Harry looked at her. What a fool she was. Even if she had not made those vows, Harry was a rake. And she was cursed!

As much as she did not want to believe it, her family was fine evidence. Not a single happy marriage between them. She only hoped Daniel and Isabel were the exception. But could she risk her heart to Harry when it would all turn out so horribly? How could she not have learned from her friends' experiences?

Harry gave the dog's head a quick ruffle. "I think I can be assured he shall keep you safe."

Suppressing a sigh, she forced attention on the dog. Bringing her a loyal pet and smiling at her like that...how was she meant to resist?

"You need not worry over me so much, Harry."

He shook his head, his gaze intense when she peeked up. "I must, Merry. I really must."

Lord, the look in his eyes...the timbre of his voice. It all had her wondering...what if Harcourt Easton, Earl of Langley really did care for her? What if, perhaps, just perhaps, he actually loved her?

Chapter Seventeen

The door to the drawing room slid open. Merry glanced up from her book at the intrusion. Orion lifted his head, giving off a slight grunt of annoyance at being disturbed. She rather felt the same. After a busy day of cleaning and dog-wrangling yesterday, she had opted for a day of reading and studying.

A day indoors with no chance of running into Harry too. A day to mull things over.

Bella entered, looking grim. Sophia and Arabella followed, their expressions and manner of walk equally miserable. Merry set her book on the armchair and stood.

"What is it? What has happened?"

Bella's throat worked, and she raised her chin. "We are calling a Spinster's Club meeting," she announced. "Sit down, Merry."

Merry sank slowly back into her chair and frowned. Her friends arranged themselves on each of the chairs surrounding the small table in the center and Merry saw glances swing between them.

"What is going on?" Merry demanded. "Why do we need to call a meeting?" She turned to Arabella. "Arabella?"

Arabella shook her head slightly. If it was nothing to do with her, then what was it? Merry could not fathom.

"Tell me what is going on." Merry pressed hands to her stomach. "You are making me nervous."

Sophia sat upright. "Well, if you two shall not say it, I will..." She licked her lips. "We came here, as members of the Spinster's Club, to warn you."

Merry leaned forward. "Warn me?"

"There has been some gossip," Arabella said softly.

"Gossip?" Merry intoned.

Bella nodded. "It's not surprising, Merry. Even we have noticed all the attention he gives you." She paused and focused on the dog. "Where did he come from?"

Merry gave Orion an affectionate rub on the head. "This is Orion. Harry brought him to me to to...to..." She couldn't quite bring herself to say to protect her. After all, it would all sound ludicrous. "To keep me company."

Bella and Sophia shared a look. Sophia motioned to the dog. "This is what we are talking about."

Merry blinked. "A dog?"

"No." Sophia shook her head. "About Harcourt."

Damn her, why did her heart have to skip at the mere mention of his name? "What about him?"

"The gossip has been about Harcourt...and you," replied Arabella quietly.

A cold wash of dread came over her. "What sort of gossip?"

Sophia laced her hands together. "I heard it from my lady's maid. Your time together has not gone unnoticed, nor has all the attention he has been paying you."

Bella nodded. "It is hard to ignore."

"We are friends," protested Merry. "We have often spent time together."

Arabella leaned over and took Merry's hand. "But you are alone, Merry, without the protection of your brother. And you must admit, he has been a lot more interested than usual. I know he likely feels he must take some sort of protective role as your brother's friend, but if it is drawing the attention of servants…"

Merry pressed fingers to her forehead and rubbed them in circles. "Then people will assume our conduct is inappropriate."

"You know I like Easton," Bella spilled out. "He's frightfully handsome and charming. But he is Harcourt Easton. He is known to be a rake. While your reputation is beyond rebuke, his is not. Any woman spending too much time with him, risks her reputation…and what concerns us more, is that she risks her heart."

Merry huffed. "As if I would risk my heart." The words felt false on her tongue. "He is a friend and I am well aware of his reputation."

"We only say these things because we do not wish to see you sent off to Ireland or some other awful place because of a man." Arabella squeezed her hand tight. "We love you too much."

Merry smiled weakly. "I love you all too."

"I was lucky no one knew of my attachment to Frederick. If anyone had realized, I'm certain my parents would have sent me away, and I certainly could not show my face in Society." Arabella fidgeted, her cheeks a little red. "I spent too long waiting for him to return, and I regret every second I wasted on him, and I certainly regret ever giving my innocence to the bloody vile man."

"Oh, bravo." Bella clapped her hands together. "That is the first time I have ever heard you call him what he is."

"Well, I think this has all made me realize what a waste of time he was." Arabella turned to face Merry. "Harcourt seems a good man, but so did Frederick. I would so hate for you to go through the same thing."

Merry patted Arabella's hand. "I have no intention of letting myself fall for him or his charms."

"Sometimes we cannot help it, but this is what the Spinster's Club is here for, is it not?" Sophia said. "So we can protect each other?"

Merry drew in a breath and nodded. "Yes, absolutely."

Her friends were right. Her time spent with Harry was inappropriate and so long as she was unsure whether his intentions were real, she could not give in. She would do her best to ignore him and avoid him until Daniel returned and she had no doubt once her brother was back, Harry's attentions would cease, and he would find someone else to amuse him. He'd most likely be back to seeing her as Daniel's little sister and nothing more. The problem would be solved, and she could return to her studies in peace and quiet.

Perfect.

Was it not?

Chapter Eighteen

"**Y**ou are always so busy these days." Harcourt's mother huffed.

Harcourt lifted his gaze from the letters in front of him and eyed his mother. She swept into the study with her usual dramatic flair, draping herself over a chair in the corner.

"In case you had not noticed, this estate takes some running."

She made a dismissive noise. "You were never that interested in the estate before. Always happy to let your men deal with it."

Harcourt lifted a brow. "Are you not happy I am taking an interest?"

She paused and considered this. "I suppose. But it does rather take you away from having fun."

What she meant was, it prevented him from spending time with the ladies she wished him to meet. The truth was between protecting Merry as best as he could and running the estate and his business dealings, he had no time or inclination to meet any of these women his mother kept thrusting at him. At some point, he would have to confess her efforts were in vain.

Not quite yet, though. His mother's need for drama would only hinder any attempts when it came to Merry—Merry did not like attention.

"I cannot win with you, Mother. You wish me to settle down and yet you complain," he teased.

She straightened in the chair. "I am glad you are taking an interest. Every mother expects their son to have a little...fun. But you did stretch out that fun for some time."

"I am sorry to have so disappointed you," he said dryly.

Smiling, she shook her head. "You mistake me, Harry. I am infinitely proud to call you my son. You are a good man and have never caused me any problems. There are some mothers who have drunks and gamblers for sons, and I am always grateful I am not one of those. A few dalliances here and there are well enough, and I could not expect anything less from having a handsome son, but I only hope your reputation does not hinder your marriage."

Too late for that. Merry's insistence he was too much of a rake for her had already hindered things. He did not regret taking the time to discover exactly what he wanted out of life, but he did regret that it was getting in the way of what he truly desired—Merry.

"Of course," his mother continued, "so many women would be willing to overlook your reputation due to your wealth and rank, but I do so want a happy marriage for you, not one of resent and bitterness."

"It is good to know you do not wish to just thrust me into the arms of whichever willing woman comes next."

She narrowed her gaze at him. "I only want what's best for you, like any mother. Your father and I had a happy marriage and I would wish the same for you."

"Well, I shall try my best."

She clapped her hands together and stood. "That is all I can ask. Well, that and one other thing..."

"What do you want?" he asked slowly.

"A ball."

He shook his head.

"We have not hosted one in a long time because you are usually in London and I am in Bath, but people are expecting one now that we are returned."

"No."

"Yes, Harry," she insisted. "It is the done thing."

"And I suppose you shall be inviting lots of eligible young ladies?"

"If eligible young ladies happen to wish to attend, who am I to stop them?" She lifted her hands.

"I am sorry to disappoint, but I do not have time to organize a ball." Not if he was to keep Merry safe. He glanced at the clock. She had agreed she would not go anywhere unescorted, but he'd wager she was at the house by now. He needed to check she had not gone alone.

"You do not need to organize it. I shall do all the work." His mother pressed a finger to her lips. "I think Saturday would be perfect. The beautiful weather looks set to continue."

He coughed. "Saturday? Mother, that is two days' away."

Straightening her shoulders, she eyed him. "Do you know me at all, Harry? In my time I arranged many a soiree within mere days and with fewer funds and less help than I have now."

Harcourt pushed aside the letters, giving her his full attention. The sooner he got this over with, the sooner he could get back to work. "You really think you can arrange a ball with such short notice?"

"Of course I bloody well can."

He chuckled. "If I say yes, will you let me work?"

"I will let you work once you've accompanied me on a ride. I need some fresh air and so do you and poor Lord Thornford."

"Riding at your age, Mother? How scandalous?"

She thrust up her nose. "I did not come here to be insulted. I came to see if my loving and loyal son would accompany his—as he so kindly pointed out—ageing mother and ensure nothing happens to her."

"That is emotional blackmail, Mother."

She grinned. "Did it work?"

He sighed and laid down his quill. "Looks like I am going for a ride."

Her triumphant grin had him shaking his head.

Apparently, his mother had requested his horse be saddled as their mounts were ready and waiting for them when they reached the stables. Griff was already saddled.

"It seems we're going for a ride," he said dryly.

"Griff, you should not let my mother bully you."

"She is rather tenacious." Griff's grin tilted.

They set off from the estate land, heading out over the hills that the house nestled on. Once they reached the outskirts of the land, signaled by a line of trees, his mother came to a stop.

"Are you done for the day, Mother?" Harcourt queried.

She glanced around. "Pardon? Oh no. I just...need to take a little rest."

Harcourt frowned. It was not like her to need a rest. Her face brightened, and he peered in the direction she was looking. Heading toward them were three women on horseback. He shared a look with Griff and grimaced. It seemed this was no simple ride but another of his mother's matchmaking attempts.

"Oh look," she said, forced surprise lighting her voice. "It is Mrs. Devine and her daughters. What a happy coincidence."

"Coincidence, my arse," Harcourt muttered, and Griff chuckled.

Pasting a smile on his face, he greeted the sisters courteously. They were a pretty couple with pleasant manners, but both were shy and clearly uncomfortable with their mother's attempts at matchmaking.

"Shall we continue on?" Harcourt suggested. It would be harder for them to converse if they were riding and would save them all from embarrassment at their mother's actions.

"Of course. Though, I think I must take it a little more slowly," his mother said. "But do not let that slow you down. Mrs. Devine can keep me company."

Harcourt rolled his eyes and set the pace again. Both girls were excellent riders and far better at it than conversing. He and Griff rode with vigor, using the countryside to show off their skills. The girls laughed and relaxed as the journey continued on.

"We had better slow down," said Harcourt. "We have lost the mothers." He slowed and glanced back to where the older women were taking their time to catch up with them.

"You are an excellent rider, my lord." Miss Charlotte smiled, her cheeks rosy from the exertion.

"As are you, Miss Charlotte." He looked to her sister. "And you, Miss Devine."

The blush in Miss Devine's cheeks deepened. "Thank you, my lord. My sister and I like to ride as often as we can."

Harcourt nodded. "But not in this direction often, I would wager."

Miss Charlotte swung a glance at her sister and grimaced. "Our mother insisted we ride out this way today. We did not fathom the reason why."

"Charlotte," hissed her younger sister. "You should not be admitting that."

Griff chuckled. "Well, I am not complaining about this meeting. Not when I get to see such beautiful women enjoying the fresh country air."

"Oh." Miss Devine's face turned nearly completely red.

"Careful, Griff," Harcourt murmured. "My mother shall have you married before dawn if you do not be cautious with your flirtations."

Their mothers were not far behind, so Harcourt gave the horse a flick with his reins and widened the gap. They rode until they reached the village then circled back around to head in the direction of the Devine's house.

"I am quite thirsty," Harcourt's mother declared once they reached the modest but elegant home.

"Oh you must come inside," Mrs. Devine said. "All of you."

Miss Charlotte rolled her eyes. Harcourt masked a chuckle. "I am afraid I have estate duties to attend to," he explained.

"But—" his mother started.

"They are quite urgent I am afraid. And I could do with a hand from Griff."

"But—" protested Griff.

"Thank you for the excellent ride, ladies. Mother, you take your time. There is no need to rush home and do send word if you need a carriage."

"I am not ancient," he heard her grumble as he and Griff lead their horses away from the house.

Harcourt shook his head. "If that is not enough to chase you back to London, I do not know what is."

Griff shrugged. "They were a little on the quiet side but charming. Not to mention excellent riders. I like a woman who can handle a horse."

"As excellent a woman as my mother is, I cannot help wish she'd return to Bath."

"And leave you to courting Miss Merry?" Griff shot a knowing look his way.

Harcourt said nothing.

"I know it is more than a passing fancy, Easton. I'm no fool."

They made their way back toward the estate at an easy pace. Harcourt had every intention of seeing Merry before the day ended but managed to resist the urge to race home to change.

"She is the reason for the change in you, is she not?" Griff pressed. "Why you no longer want to spend time in London and why you have not taken a lover in an eternity?"

"It has not been an eternity," he muttered.

"Have you asked her to marry you?"

"Not yet."

Griff peered at him. "Why the devil not?"

Harcourt stared straight ahead, ignoring his friend's inquisitive stare. "Let's just say Merry is not convinced that I am the marrying type."

Griff laughed. "She has turned you down?"

"Not as such." He sighed. "But she is refusing to let herself admit she wants me."

"It sounds like she is going to take some persuading."

Harcourt nodded and tightened his grip on the reins. "Indeed. A fine job I do not give up easily."

"First you have to figure out who is trying to hurt her," Griff pointed out. "Can hardly seduce her while trying to protect her."

Harcourt gave his friend a look and Griff laughed. "You devil, you have been trying to do both."

"It is more than seduction with Merry," Harcourt admitted. "I love the woman, Griff."

Griff shook his head slowly. "Well, I do not know her that well yet, but she seems to be quite the woman. I cannot say I see why you would wish to settle already but if there's any woman that can keep you on your toes, it will be her."

"I have a private investigator I can call on for help. He was unable to discover anything previously, but things have developed since then."

"So with any luck, you shall find out who is trying to harm her. But what will you do about the marriage thing?" Griff asked.

Harcourt gave the reins a flick and sent the horse into a gallop. "You know me, Griff," he said. "I have never been one to give up easily."

Chapter Nineteen

"No, you need to lift it at that corner," Sophia ordered, bending down to demonstrate lifting the corner of the huge painting.

"I think I know perfectly well how to lift a painting," Bella grumbled.

Merry grimaced. Today was meant to have been nice and easy. All they need to do was hang a few paintings. But Bella and Sophia were determined to argue over everything they did today.

Orion darted into the room, racing around Sophia then brushing past Merry before heading into one of the other rooms. She shook her head. Orion did not want them to make much progress either apparently.

"Why do we not take a quick break?" Merry suggested.

Arabella returned to the bedroom. "I've hung that smaller one. Do you want to take a look?"

"In a moment. Let's move this big one," said Sophia.

"I was talking to Merry actually," said Arabella softly.

"Let's move this one first so that Sophia and Bella can stop arguing," suggested Merry.

Sophia scowled. "We are not arguing."

"You were," said Bella.

"It was you who was doing all the shouting," shot back Sophia.

Shaking her head, Merry stepped forward. "Why don't Arabella and I do it instead? You two can take those two smaller ones downstairs." She motioned to two she had selected to hang in the hallway.

"We can manage." Bella lifted her corner of the painting.

"Yes, we're not incapable, Merry." Sophia bent down to snatch up her end, but she lifted it too quickly and the painting slid from Bella's grasp, the corner crashing down on Bella's toes.

Bella let out a pained yelp and hopped back, grabbing her injured foot.

Arabella hastened forward. "Oh no, are you hurt?"

"I've probably broken my toe thanks to Sophia." Bella sent a daggered look Sophia's way.

Sophia folded her arms. "You should have had a better grip."

"It wasn't my fault either. You have big, clumsy man hands."

Sophia sucked in an outraged gasp. "I do not. You're the one with huge hands. Look at those big ugly things!"

Merry pressed fingers to her temples and drew in a long breath. If they could not even move paintings without getting into some kind of disaster, what hope did they have of ever finishing clearing the house without anyone's help?

Arabella stepped forward and held up her hands. "You're upsetting, Merry," she said softly.

Bella and Sophia glanced at her. Sophia grimaced. "Forgive me, Merry. I did not sleep well and I'm feeling grumpy."

"No doubt it's because you were snoring all night. Arabella, said as much, did you not?" Bella folded her arms across her chest.

"Bella," warned Arabella.

She rolled her eyes. "Fine, I am sorry. Even though you do snore a little."

Sophia narrowed her gaze. "So do you. If I have big, clumsy man hands, you snore like a man who's passed out after a great meal and vast quantities of sherry."

Merry held her breath while Bella's face reddened a little. She could feel the tears burning behind her eyes. Why did everything seem too hard suddenly? Why did everything feel like a battle? Even Harry. Each meeting with him, she felt like she had to raise the defenses and man the moat. Everything had become so complicated suddenly.

Most especially her feelings toward him.

A sudden peal of laughter escaped Bella. She drew in a breath and clamped her lips together until the giggles were suppressed. "I am sorry. Truly. And Sophia is right. I do snore like a drunken man—especially when I have had a sherry myself."

Sophia perfected a smug look.

"It just all seemed a little amusing for a moment. Arguing over paintings and all the disasters we have come across. Perhaps your family curse is nothing to do with marriage," she said to Merry. "Perhaps this house is cursed."

"Merry is not cursed," Arabella declared. "In any way at all. Not when it comes to marriage, nor when it comes to this house. We just have to try a little harder, that is all. We shall get it finished and you can finally have your little escape away from the world."

Merry gave a soft smile. At the moment, nothing appealed to her more than the idea of being able to tuck herself away in this house away from the estate and housekeepers who interfered in her life too much, and men who wanted to send her into a tizzy every time she saw them.

"Come on, let us get back to work." Sophia snatched up the end of the painting once more. "If we get these hung, we can eat that lavender shortbread my cook made. That must be incentive enough."

"Oh yum." Bella rubbed her stomach. "I do wish father would hire a new cook. Mrs. Hitchens is a grumpy old bat."

"She has been with the family for nearly twenty years, Bella," reminded Arabella.

Bella lifted her chin. "That does not mean she is any good as a cook. I think I could do a better job." She motioned to Merry. "Remember when you came for afternoon tea and she burnt the cakes and gave us spoiled milk."

Merry grimaced. "That milk was a little rancid."

"You sound spoiled, Bella," Sophia warned.

Bella lifted her nose into the air. "And you sound like Mrs. Hitchens. The woman loathes me, I swear."

"Because you are spoiled and outrageous," said Sophia. "Now are you going to help me with this painting or not."

Bella paused, a glint in her eyes. "Well, I do not know. If I am so spoiled, I am not sure I am the sort to be doing heavy lifting."

Merry wrapped an arm around Bella's shoulders. "Whether you are spoiled or not, we love you just the way you are."

"You are only saying that so that I get on with the work." Bella grinned.

"Perhaps." Merry chuckled. Leave it to Bella to help her forget all her frustrations. "Did it work?"

She bent down to pick up the other corner of the painting. "I am an absolute pushover for flattery. Of course it worked!"

Merry and Arabella snatched up a few of the smaller paintings and followed Sophia and Bella downstairs into the drawing room. Orion raced past Merry, excited by all the movement, down the corridor then back into the room. The large painting was propped up against the wall while Merry spread out the smaller ones to study them.

"I was thinking I would have that large one on that wall." She pointed to the wall opposite the window. "Then the smaller ones here."

Arabella stepped back to eye the room and nodded. "That sounds perfect." She looked at Merry. "I confess I am a little jealous of you setting up home on your own."

"There is something to be said to living alone," Sophia admitted.

"I would rather not have to gain a horrible husband before doing it, though," pointed out Bella.

Sophia grimaced. "I like my freedom as a widow, and I am grateful for what I inherited from him. *But* I would not wish such a miserable match on anyone."

"Let us just be grateful he dropped dead so quickly!" Bella said. "Just think you could have been stuck with him for another couple of decades."

Arabella gasped. "Bella, you should not speak ill of the dead."

Bella's lips twisted. "I will more than happily speak ill of that beast. He mistreated Sophia."

Sophia held up her hands. "It is fine. I have made my peace with it all now. But I cannot claim to be sad he passed."

"If I had known at the time, I'd have killed him myself," Bella said between gritted teeth.

None of them had been aware Sophia's husband was mistreating her during their marriage. He made sure they rarely saw her and remained in London most of the time. It was not until after her husband's death, did Sophia admit how awful he was to her. Two years had passed since then, and for the most part, Sophia seemed utterly at peace with it all. Merry was not convinced those sorts of scars could heal that easily, however, but she was loath to bring it up unless Sophia did.

Merry nodded. "I think we all would have done him some harm, had we known."

Holding both hands up, Sophia shook her head. "What's done is done."

"Now, talking of men. Your mama said she saw Easton riding with the Devine sisters." Bella nodded toward Sophia and Arabella. "It seems the dowager countess is angling for a match with one of them."

Merry grimaced. She did not want to hear this. She did not want to think about Harry with other women. Curling her hands at her side, she managed to resist clapping her hands over her ears.

"They shall be lucky to secure him," Arabella commented. "Everyone knows what a rake he is."

Bella shrugged. "Your mama said he looked to be enjoying himself."

Merry's heart sank further. She'd been right about him, but that did not mean she liked being correct.

Sophia tutted. "I do not know why you listen to our mother. She is always gossiping, and it is rarely correct. Now, are we going to hang these paintings or not?"

"Let us get that big one over and done with," Bella suggested. "Then perhaps it shall land on no more toes."

"Yes," agreed Merry. "Once that one is up, we can see what the room shall look like and then we can figure out where the rest go."

Bella and Sophia lifted it once more, easing it up while Merry wrangled it over the picture hooks.

"Anyone home?"

Merry's heart juddered to a stop at the sound of the baritone echoing around the house.

"Oh it's..." Bella stopped as soon as Merry clapped a hand over her mouth. Bella made a muffled protest against her hand.

"Do not say anything," hissed Merry. "I do not want to see him."

"Why ever not?" asked Arabella.

"I...I just do not." Merry straightened. "I...I'm fed up with him always checking up on me. I am perfectly capable of looking after myself."

Footsteps echoed down the hallway and Orion barked, dashing off in the direction of the sound before Merry could grab him.

"Blast." She swung her gaze about the room then darted behind one of the long, velvet curtains that had recently been cleaned and rehung.

Arabella peeled back one edge of the curtain. "What are you doing, Merry?"

"Hiding. *Shh*." She pressed a finger to her lip. "Tell Harry I am not here. I've gone into the village or something." Merry snatched back the curtain and tucked it around herself, holding her breath when those heavy footsteps entered the room.

She closed her eyes and willed herself to remain still. She could not face him, not after everything that had occurred between them recently—not to mention all the gossip surrounding them. It was all too much. If she saw him...well, she feared she might crumble. And where would that leave her? With a broken heart and no friends probably.

"Good afternoon, ladies," she heard him say.

"Good afternoon, my lord," replied Arabella. "What brings you here?"

"I was hoping to see Merry," he said.

"Oh. Um." Arabella tripped over a response and Merry grimaced.

"She isn't here!" Bella cut in. "She has gone..."

"To the village," finished Sophia. "To get some..."

"Bonnets!" put in Bella.

Merry grimaced and pressed fingers between her brows.

"Bonnets?" queried Harcourt.

"Yes," Arabella said, a breathless quality to her voice. "I, um, ruined mine while we were tidying, so Merry just felt so guilty she had to replace it straight away."

"I see." Footsteps creaked around the perimeter of the room. Merry sucked in a breath once more and held it until they receded.

"Is she alone?" Harry asked.

Silence hung in the room. Merry's heartbeat was so loud, she could swear he had to be able to hear it.

"After the other day, she should not be going anywhere alone." There was annoyance in his tone.

"I am sure she shall be fine. She has only gone to the village after all," said Bella brightly.

"She did not even take Orion," he mused.

"Well, Mrs. Bryce would never let him in her shop. She detests animals of all kinds," Sophia put in.

Merry smiled at this. It wasn't a lie but thank goodness Sophia had recalled that snippet of information.

"I am glad I found you all anyway. With the exception of Merry." Suspicion edged his voice. "My mother has decreed there shall be a ball in two days' time. I hope you shall all attend."

"Will there be food and sherry?" Bella asked.

"Naturally," Harry replied.

"Excellent. So long as you do not expect me to dance, I will happily attend," Bella said.

"Would you not even spare me a dance?" Harry asked.

Merry curled her fist. Something strange fisted in her gut at the idea of Harry dancing with other ladies. Even Bella. Which was ridiculous. Bella would never fall for Harry's charm, even if she thought him handsome. Of course, she would not be able to attend the ball, considering she was still in mourning so she would not even have to witness Harry taking other women in his arms.

Even if she did, it would not matter, she reminded herself. Because she simply did not care who Harry took in his arms. The sooner he moved his attentions onto someone else, the better, was that not right?

She missed the rest of the conversation, only realizing Harry had left when Arabella whipped the curtain open, making Merry clap hands across her chest and suck in a breath. She scanned the room and realized he had truly gone before letting herself sag a little.

"What on earth was that about, Merry?" Arabella asked. "We seemed awfully silly, and I do not like lying."

"I am an excellent liar." Bella grinned. "But you two made it all worse."

Sophia gave Bella a stern look. "Being good at lying is not something to be proud of. But you did no better than the rest of us."

Merry sunk down onto a chair, aware of the looks her friends were giving her. She should tell them. They were her friends after all. She should admit that Harry made her heart race and her body feel as though it had somehow been separated from her and she was entirely out of control when it came to Harry.

But how could she? She had started the Spinsters Club after all. It had all been her idea. And had they not just been discussing Sophia's awful late-husband? How would she feel if she knew Merry had been...

Had been falling for Harry.

There, she could not avoid the admission. She had been falling for him since he put his lips to hers. Maybe for longer. It was hard to tell now. She'd always admired him and thought him handsome and charming. Perhaps even when she'd been younger, she'd fallen for him just a little.

And he was all too aware of that. If she even admitted as much, he would swoop in and claim his victory before leaving her heartbroken. She simply could not confess as much, not even to her closest friends.

"We just had a little falling out," said Merry hastily. "Just a little falling out."

She could tell none of them were convinced but she did not have the energy to try to convince them. How could she when she could not even convince herself that falling for Harry was the worst conceivable idea ever?

Chapter Twenty

"Harry!"

Harcourt turned sharply on his heel and pushed through a mass of bodies before his mother could catch up with him. If only the bloody woman would stop forcing him to dance with every young lady of her choosing. Though there were some pretty and sweet ladies in attendance, he'd rather pick his own matches.

He'd rather pick Merry.

"Harry!" There was a tug on his arm and he sighed before turning to face his mother. How the woman managed to force her way through the filled ballroom to catch up with him, he did not know. "You are to dance with Miss Eloise Burton now." She gave his arm a tug.

"I am quite capable of choosing my own partners, Mother."

She lifted a brow. "Are you? Because I think if I left you to it, you would not choose anyone." She tilted her head, making the feathers tucked into her hair bounce. "Are you unwell, Harry? Because even in your more...roguish days, you always enjoyed a dance."

"I still enjoy a dance. Just not with every woman in the entire country under the age of twenty-two."

His mother pressed her lips together. "I did not invite every woman in the country."

He glanced around at the crowded room. It was not the first ball to be held at Lulworth Castle and would not be the last but considering his mother had put it together in a mere two days, it was quite an event. Suffice to say, the servants had been at the point of rebellion, having to cater to so many guests at the last minute. It had taken a few choice words and promises of days off to ensure things continued to run smoothly.

Of course, the one person he wished to be here, could not be. Not that she'd be wanting to dance. He'd probably find Merry tucked up in a room somewhere with a book or hiding in the gardens. He was beginning to wonder if she might not have the right idea, though he would not complain about being forced to take her in his arms.

"You did an impressive job, Mother, so why do you not go and enjoy yourself rather than worrying about your grown son?"

"You really do not understand mothers at all, do you? It is my job to worry about you."

Harcourt leaned in and gave her a kiss on the cheek. "And I appreciate it. Why do you not find Lord Thornford a lovely partner?" He peered at his friend who was enjoying the company of an elegant fair-haired young lady. "Anyway, I have already decided on my next dance partner. He scanned the room and settled his gaze on Bella Lockhart. She glanced his way and stilled as he strolled over. "Will you dance the next set with me?"

Creases appeared between her brows. Dressed in fine white silk, Bella was a far cry from the slightly dusty and grimy woman he'd seen a few days ago at the dower house. She gave a little curtsey. "Of course, my lord. Though I must warn you I have a tendency to tread on people's toes."

Harcourt grinned. "It is a fine job I am wearing sturdy boots then."

Once the next set was called—an English Country Dance—he led Bella up to the dance floor and stood at the head of the line while they waited for the music to start up.

"Are you having an enjoyable time?" he asked Bella.

"Of course. You certainly know how to put on a ball."

"I cannot take all the credit I am afraid. The dowager countess did most of the work." They began the dance, weaving around the other dancers before stopping. "I did not think you were one to enjoy balls, Bella. Much like Merry."

She shook her head. "Formal balls are a bore. And this is of course, a formal ball," she hastened to add. "but so much more relaxed than London balls. At least all my friends are here."

"With the exception of Merry."

Bella narrowed her gaze at him. "I know you are good friends, my lord, but you are spending an uncommon amount of time together. You are putting her reputation at risk."

"Well, I have not seen her for several days if that puts your mind at ease. In fact, I did not even manage to catch up with her after her strange disappearing act at the dower house."

A blush bloomed on Bella's cheeks. "There was nothing strange about it. She had to go fetch some new hanging hooks."

He let his lips slant. "I thought it was bonnets."

"Oh, yes. Bonnets too!" she said hurriedly.

They made their way back down the line, lacing their hands together then loosening them.

"Where is Merry tonight?" he asked once they had come to a stop.

Bella shook her head with a small smile. "You will not be dissuaded will you, my lord?"

"It's my duty to look out for her while her brother is gone."

"A duty makes it sound tiresome. I think you enjoy looking out for her."

He shrugged. "Perhaps I do."

"I think perhaps she enjoys you looking out for her more than she will admit." She grinned.

The words made his heart warm. If her good friend saw that Merry had feelings for him, then surely it was only a matter of time before Merry gave up this ridiculous fight to avoid him.

"So do you know where she is tonight?" he pressed.

"At the dower house, I suspect. She mentioned something about using the time alone to arrange her books."

Harcourt shook his head. If she was all alone in the house, she could be in danger. But with luck, the man he had stationed to watch over her had followed her. He'd brought the private investigator back on to follow her and ensure she remained safe when he could not. It still did not stop him from wanting to check on her, however.

"Thank you for the dance, Miss Bella. And thank you for not damaging my toes."

She chuckled. "You were one of the lucky ones."

He excused himself and made his way across the ballroom. Griff stopped in front of him, loosening the hold of a determined young woman on his arm who moved dejectedly away.

"Where are you off to in such a rush, Easton? I saw you dancing with that Lockhart woman. She's an attractive thing. Might see if I can't get a dance myself."

A cough from behind Harcourt made him turn. Bella Lockhart eyed Griff, her hands to her hips. "I am no thing. Nor am I 'that Lockhart woman', my lord. You shall not be getting a dance from me tonight nor any other night."

With that, Bella spun on her heel and vanished into the crowds. Harcourt chuckled at this friend's bewildered expression.

"Well, damn, a lady would never talk like that in London."

Harcourt shook his head. "You deserved it, Griff."

"I suppose I had better rustle up another partner instead."

Grinning, Harcourt nodded toward his mother. "Not to fear, my mother shall have someone lined up for you."

Griff grimaced.

"I thought you rather enjoyed having all these country ladies clamoring for you," said Harcourt.

"I think I changed my mind." Griff scanned the room. "Perhaps I can persuade Bella Lockhart to give me another chance."

Harcourt shook his head. "You are a glutton for punishment."

Griff's smile expanded. "That I am. Where are you running to anyway? You did not say."

"Do I need to?"

Griff rolled his eyes. "Lady Merry, of course. Well, not to fear, I shall keep your mother occupied while you hunt down your elusive love interest."

"You are an excellent friend, Griff. I won't ever forget it." Harcourt clapped a hand on Griff's shoulder before leaving the ballroom and heading outside.

Chapter Twenty-One

Merry ran a finger along the gold lettering on the spine of the book before placing it carefully on the bookshelf. Sat on the cold floor with books scattered around her, her only company was Orion and his whistling snore. Every now and then, his ears would perk up at the sound of a dripping tap or one of the many creaks in the house, but apparently it was far too late for him to get up to mischief, so he had opted to spend most of the evening curled on the rug by the fireplace.

She glanced over at the empty fireplace. The evenings were too warm for fires but once summer was behind them, the study would be lovely once lit by the glow of a fire—the perfect place to continue her translation.

She rubbed Orion's head and grabbed the next book from one of the many piles scattered about the room. She should be at the main house at this time of night, but she had Orion here to protect her. Harry would probably still have a fit. However, she needed to keep busy.

Not that she minded missing the ball. Of course she did not. Balls had always bored her. Few men ever asked her to dance and even if they did, they quickly discovered her dancing skills were almost non-existent. Most balls were either spent with her friends, tucked away where they would not have to be wallflowers or hiding somewhere alone with a book.

Much like this evening, she supposed.

A tight knot bunched in her throat as she imagined everyone gathered together in a bright ballroom, chandeliers glinting overhead and strains of music whispering through the air. She shoved the book onto the bookcase and snatched up the next. She hoped her friends were having fun. Really she did. And Harry. So what if he was dancing with eligible young ladies? That was a good thing, was it not? Perhaps his attention would be transferred to someone else and she could escape this awful turmoil besieging her when it came to him.

Merry grimaced. Who was she kidding? Even if she was to be a wallflower, she'd rather be at the ball than alone. With Daniel gone and the passing of her father, it did not matter that she had the support of her friends. She really was utterly alone—especially when she could not admit to them the truth of her feelings toward Harry.

Vision blurring, she sniffed and smoothed a hand over Orion's head. The soft texture of his fur, instead of soothing her, made the tears fall down her cheeks. She was silly to cry—especially over men. Over her father and Harry.

Her father, in particular, would have told her to stop being a silly girl. Would he even care that she mourned him? Probably not. It had been clear since she'd first had some kind of understanding of how a father should be that he saw her as nothing more than a nuisance—an extension of him that disappointed. On the rare occasions he acknowledged her existence, it was with frustration and scorn.

Merry drew in a breath. How silly she was, crying over that man—or any man for that matter. The Spinster Club would not be impressed with her.

A thud from outside the room made her heart give a little leap. Orion lifted his head and cocked it, his ears raised.

"You heard that too?" she whispered.

She stood. It could have been nothing. The house was prone to noises and they were even more pronounced at night while she was alone. But she could not help think of Harry and his concerns for her. What if it was whoever was trying to harm her? Oh dear, Harry would be aggravated indeed if he knew she'd ignored his warnings. Just her luck to run into trouble while everyone is at the ball, enjoying themselves.

Easing out of the door, she made her way down the corridor to the source of the thud. Book in hand, she wielded it like a weapon, ready to strike. The house was dark. The only candles were lit in the study and little light emanated from there now she was farther into the depths of the house. Her mouth dried and her heart beat painfully hard. What would she do if she found an intruder? Beat him senseless? Tie him up perhaps? Find out why on earth this person was trying to hurt her.

Orion crept alongside her, apparently aware of the need for quiet. She had to surprise whoever it was if she wanted to defeat him.

A shadow loomed, another thud echoed. Merry held her breath and lunged forward, swinging the book with all her might. It connected with a body and there was a grunt of pain. Orion barked and dashed forward then stopped. Merry lifted her book, freezing as silvery evening light silhouetted the intruder. She released all the air from her lungs.

"Harry?"

"Yes." He gave a groan. "What a fine welcome."

"Oh no." She grabbed his arm and lead him through into the study. Dressed in full finery, he struck a handsome figure, even with what looked to be a bruise forming on his forehead. She urged him over to the chair to sit down.

Orion looked contrite for his part in the attack and settled himself at Harry's feet.

"Who knew books were so dangerous?" Harry looked pointedly at the book in her hand.

She set it hastily aside and pushed a lock of hair away from his forehead. "Some would say books were very dangerous, particularly to women's minds."

"I do not suppose any of those men who declared such a thing considered they could be just as dangerous in a woman's hands."

"I am sorry. I thought you were an intruder." She lifted a candle and inspected the damage closer. "Why are you not at the ball?"

"I must have had an instinct that you were getting into trouble."

"Well, as you can see, I'm not in any trouble at all." He winced when she pressed fingers to the red mark on his head. "At least I was not until you turned up." She eyed the mark. "I think this shall bruise. You really should not have been sneaking around in the dark. Will everyone not miss you?"

He shrugged. "Perhaps. But there will be plenty more balls to attend in future, I'm sure."

The thought of Harry dancing at more balls with yet more women made her heart twist.

She turned away. "I should find something cool to ease the swelling."

Harry grabbed her wrist. "No."

She let her eyes widen at his sudden touch. The feel of his warm fingers on her skin sent a shudder through her. The air around her stilled when she met his gaze. Even Orion must have felt it. From the corner of her eye, she saw the dog lift his head then turn away from them to close his eyes and settle.

A noose of tension tightened around her throat. She gave an experimental tug on his grip and found herself going nowhere. She was not sure if she could anyway. He had her captive. His gaze searched hers and he stood.

Damn him, why did he have to look so handsome in his finery? Why did he have to find her at this most vulnerable moment? But then, had she not been vulnerable since the first time he'd kissed her. He'd had her set off kilter since then, warring with herself against these feelings that would not seem to be pushed away, no matter what the stakes.

Your heart, that voice whispered. That was what was at risk. But that blasted whisper merely sounded eager, as though it wanted her to give it up to him once and for all. There was no denying it—Harry had been a feature in her life for too long for her to dismiss him fully. Yes, he was a rogue. Yes, he was far too charming for his own good. But who had been there for her since her father's death? And even before that.

"Harry," she whispered, answering her own question.

He tugged her close. Her limbs were warm, and she could feel the heat rise into her face at the feel of his body flush against hers. He lifted a hand and pressed it to her cheek. She could not help lean into the touch. It eased the empty ache that had been building tonight, as though his very presence could fill her up, could complete her. The thought was terrifying.

And too enticing. Merry closed her eyes.

Harry laced his fingers into her hair. She could feel the hotness of his breath near her cheek as he used the hold he had on her to gently tilt her head upward.

"Balls do not interest me," he murmured. "How could they? Not when I could be holding you in my arms." He gave a soft chuckle. "You have ruined me, Merry."

Ruined. The word should terrify her. Ruination was the one thing that kept them all captive to Society and its whims. A ruined woman was no one. Yet the thought that she might hold such control over Harry sent a warm frisson of power through her. The feeling was fleeting, however. He reminded her who wielded the power by skimming the back of his other hand across her cheek. She felt each bumpy knuckle dancing over her skin with such reverence that her heart swelled to the point she feared it might explode or crack in half—such was the power he held over her.

She should not be allowing him such liberties. She should not even be alone with him. It was all so dangerous.

And enticing.

Her lips parted of their own accord. Harry slid a finger over her bottom lip, then traced the curve of the top. She could resist no longer and opened her eyes. His gaze was dark and intense. She was hard pressed to remember ever seeing such a look before. Could it be true? Could he really care for her as much as he had declared? Could she—plain, frizzy haired, bookish she—really inspire such desire in a man like Harry?

He brought his mouth down to hover above hers. Her lids fluttered closed once more. His breath and the very nearness of him skittered across her mouth. His lips landed first on the corner of her lips. A startled sound escaped her when a hot flush raced through her at this first minor touch.

His lips left hers and skimmed her jaw line, tracing a path to her ear. He took her lobe between his teeth and Merry gripped his arms as shivers ran their fingers up and down her spine. Her knees threatened to buckle, and she gripped him tighter.

He lavished attention on her ear, the curve of her neck, her collarbone, all the while using his hand in her hair to direct her to his will. He pressed warm kisses to her forehead, down her nose, across her cheeks. Her breaths came in hot pants. If he was intending to drive her mad, he was succeeding. Every part of her ached with need. She wanted more of these hot, sensuous kisses but she craved nothing more than his mouth upon hers.

He moaned when she used her grip to pull him tighter against her. Both hands thrust into her hair with increased vigor. His mouth finally found hers and he kissed her with determination, as though resolved to imprint himself on her forever. He needn't have worried. The first time he had kissed her was enough. Since then, she had been weak for him.

And boy oh boy was she weak for him now. Her legs trembled at the first sweep of his tongue. He kept her held firmly while he explored the depths of her mouth. She tasted his tongue, her body a whirl of sensation. His lips were firm, his tongue searching. She felt every inch of his firm body, including his arousal. Her body pulsed in response to the realization that she was summoning such desire in him.

One hand left her hair and skimmed down her side. It came around to cup her rear and she gasped as she found herself angled against his hardness with even more persistence. Merry slipped her hands up and gripped his neck, keeping him firm against her.

"Merry," he murmured briefly against her lips before delving deeper.

She stumbled back under the onslaught, taking him with her. Her bottom hit the writing desk by the window and something fell to the floor. Harry lifted her bodily onto the desk and eased himself between her legs. She sucked in a breath and stared up at him. Their gazes locked. She could see his chest rise and fall. The golden candlelight made his gaze darker than ever. It brought out each line in his face, the etchings of his experience, everything that had made Harry the man he was today.

If this were a different situation, she'd want to run her fingers across his face and feel each line and talk of life but not today. Today, she could only think of feeling *more*. More Harry, more desire, more sensation. She'd spent too long thinking. Too many years and months and weeks thinking. For once in her life, she only wanted to feel.

He cupped her cheek and gripped her rear, notching his arousal against her through the layers of fabric between them. She moaned.

He wasted no time in bringing his mouth down upon hers. The heat built once more and increased as he rocked against her. Sweet sensations built between her legs and she could only hold on, powerless, as he kissed and rocked and kissed and rocked until the feelings crested and washed over her. She shuddered in his arms and he gentled his kisses, shifting them from her mouth to her cheek then her forehead. He finally rested his forehead against hers, stroking a thumb across her cheeks while his other hand rubbed soothingly up and down her back.

Finally, he drew away. A slight smile pulled at his lips, but his gaze was troubled. "I did not mean for that to happen, Merry." He drew in shaky breath and pushed a hand through his hair. "You have a tendency to make me lose my mind."

She readjusted her skirts about her but could not bring herself to stand yet. If she did, her legs would probably give way. Her blood still flowed warm, but it was slowly being replaced with cold shock at what she'd done. If he had wanted to, he could have probably taken her. All her principles would have been swept away. She swallowed hard.

"I think...I think you should leave."

A furrow appeared between his brows. "I did not come here to seduce you."

"Did you not?"

"I came to ensure you were safe. You cannot ask me to leave now."

"I have to. I cannot let this..." She waved a hand between them, "keep happening." She stood and straightened her shoulders, hoping she looked stronger than she felt.

"Why?"

"You know why."

"I do not. You talk of my past, of my behavior. Men can change, can they not? Surely you have seen the change in me, Merry. You're the one responsible."

"I'm not sure I want that responsibility." The words were a lie. Oh, how easy it would be to give herself up to him and let herself believe it all.

"Merry, I know you too well. Do not fib to me."

"Harry, there are too many reasons..."

"You have given me one. One that I will disprove over and over again, year after year, if you let me."

Lord, how her heart fluttered at the idea. How wonderful it would be to receive his kisses...and more...for the rest of her days, to share in his life, to always have him by her side. It was a dream that was too good to be true.

"I...it's the curse too," she spilled out, unsure if she needed to convince him or herself. "And other things," she finished quietly.

"The curse?" A laugh burst out of him. "You mean the gypsy curse?"

She folded her arms and lifted her chin. "Our family has never had a happy marriage."

He shook his head. "You are too logical to believe in curses. You're using it as an excuse." He moved close, making her back up against the desk again.

She held up a palm. "My friends," she blurted. "I cannot."

"Your friends?"

She bit down on her lip and lifted her gaze to his. "I promised them. I promised them I would remain...a spinster."

"Why the devil would you promise such a thing?"

"Because they are my friends. Because they needed me. Because..." She twined her hands into her skirt fabric. "You would not understand. You are a man."

"You're right. I do not understand. What sort of friends would deny you happiness and love?"

"They have not denied me anything." She lifted her chin. "They have no idea what has happened...between us."

She whispered the last words, fearful of saying them too loud. If she admitted it aloud, it might seal them together forever, and then what? She would probably get her heart broken and her friends would be so upset with her. The Spinster's Club was all her idea after all. What sort of a friend would she be if she gave up on it already?

Harry eyed her and sighed. "I'm not giving up on you, Merry."

She blinked at him. "You should."

"I do not suppose you shall let me walk you home."

Merry folded her arms across her chest. She could not decide whether she was glad or not that he had yet to give up on her. After all, if he did not, it would mean more of his kisses, more of his attention. It was foolish of her to want more. She would only have to fight against her feelings again.

"I am going to stay here tonight."

"Lock the doors and check the windows. Anyone could get in." He grinned. "As lethal as you are with books, I do not fancy your chances against someone more determined."

"More determined than you?"

"You know what I mean." He leaned in and kissed her on the cheek before she could back away. "I shall see you tomorrow."

"Or you could stay home."

He gave her a look that she knew meant she had more chance of holding back the tide. "I'm still responsible for your safety."

She opened her mouth to protest but he left the room before she could summon a response. Sagging back against the desk, she touched a finger to her lips, feeling their swollen warmth. Somehow, she'd have to steel herself further against him. Goodness knows how she would manage that after what had just happened. As hard as she tried, Harcourt Easton had pried inside her heart and embedded himself there. It would take more than books to keep him at bay.

Chapter Twenty-Two

A fresh chill blew in from the sea, bringing with it the scent of sea salt. The day was clear, however. Perfect for taking Merry out of the damned house and putting an end to this charade. Harcourt had had a night to sleep on it—a restless night at that—and he wasn't going to back down, despite this spinster nonsense. He understood, and admired Merry's loyalty to her friends, but he had no doubt they would not deny her a chance at love.

And she damn well loved him. Yesterday's reaction had proved that, even if he did not know it already. It was not just her passion, it was the way she looked at him, the way she responded to him. More than that it was the regret shining clear in her gaze when she told him of all the reasons they could not be together. He'd understood her reticence due to his reputation, but he was certain they'd moved past that now. Surely she saw him for what he was now? A man transformed—and transformed by her.

He followed the road toward the house. If Merry had stayed overnight at the house, she'd still be there. Alone, hopefully. He wondered if she realized someone had been watching over her all night. She'd be aggravated but he did not give two hoots. Her safety was more important than whether she was annoyed with him or not.

It was still early and most of those who had been at the ball had not left until sunrise flickered over the horizon. His mother had only taken to bed a few hours ago. He should be tired, but a new energy burst through him as he saw the chimneys of the dower house. Whatever protests she came up with now, he'd shoot them down. He'd kiss her and kiss her until she climaxed in his arms again. Now that he'd had a taste of her passion, he would not relinquish her.

Not far from the house, he paused. The sound of hammering echoed through the air. He scowled. It could be the carpenter he supposed. His heart jerked a little, despite his own reassurances. He increased his pace again. This issue of someone trying to hurt her still was not resolved and he could not help fear...

"You're a fool," he muttered to himself.

Damned right. A fool for her. It was just the carpenter. He knew that as soon as he saw planks of wood piled up outside the house. The problem was, he would not be assured until he saw her. If anything ever happened to her...

He came to a stop again when a man came out of the house. And he was most certainly not the carpenter.

Another man followed him, then another. They moved the planks of wood inside and another brandished a paintbrush.

"What the devil..."

Merry came around the side of the house. He was not sure how she did it but even in dark gray and probably about as much sleep as he, she looked radiant. Her curls were a little mussed. It reminded him of how she'd looked after he'd pushed his fingers into her hair. She smiled. And not at him.

Harcourt curled a fist. She smiled up at one of the men he did not recognize as she motioned to the house. The man smiled back, and Harcourt tightened his fist until his knuckles hurt.

"What's going on?" he demanded, striding over and eyeing the man.

"Oh, Harry. I have enlisted some help," she said breezily.

How she tried to avoid his gaze did not pass by his notice. The bloody woman was determined to cut him out, he could see that, but it would take more than a few men to get rid of him.

"Have you no regard for your safety?" he hissed, taking her arm and pulling her aside.

"What on earth do you mean?"

"Do you know any of these men?"

She peered at him. "They come highly recommended from Mr. Nicholson. I hardly think any of them would have a reason to harm me." She drew up her shoulders. "Besides, I am not convinced I'm in any danger."

"Damn it, Merry—" He paused when a figure caught his eye. His heart slammed into his chest.

"Harry?"

Racing over to the new stranger, he snatched the gangly looking fellow by his shirt and shoved him up against the stone wall of the house. "What do you want with her?" he demanded.

The older man, his gray hair wild about his face, struggled to release himself from Harry's grip. "I say..."

Harcourt wasn't fooled by the act. He'd recognize the man anywhere. "This is the man who was snooping around the house. He broke into the house," he told Merry who had raced to his side.

"I certainly did not!" the stranger managed to squeak out.

"Why are you here? What do you want with Merry?" Harcourt pushed the man's frail frame harder to the wall.

"Harry!" Merry protested. "You are hurting him."

Harcourt looked at the man's reddened face and eased his grip a little. The man was no good to him if he passed out. Harcourt wanted answers.

"I promise you...I did not break anything..." The man pulled feebly against Harry's hand.

"Release him." Merry tugged at Harcourt's arm. "He cannot do any harm, look at him. Harry, please, let him go."

Harcourt glanced at Merry and eased his grip. "Fine." He thrust a finger at the man. "But one wrong move and I will kill you."

The man's pale blue eyes widened. "I-I-I do not know what you mean by wrong move. I only wanted to see my r-r-relation but I..." His face flushed red. "I well..." He thrust out a shaking hand to Harcourt. "Sir Seton at your service."

Merry frowned. "Seton? Relation?"

Sir Seton adjusted his cravat and nodded, sucking in a breath. He glanced around at the audience of workers that had gathered. "Do you...do you mind if we take this somewhere private?" He dropped his voice to nearly a whisper. "I am not...n-n-not very good with p-p-people around."

Harcourt gave Merry a look. "Surely you are not convinced by this?" He motioned to the man. Whatever this awkward, uncomfortable act was, he was not falling for it. Ever since Harcourt had spotted him outside Merry's house, all sorts of things had befallen her.

Merry eyed the man, then Harcourt. "Let us take this inside." Harcourt hesitated, and she gave him a stern look. "Harry?"

He backed away just enough to let the man slip past him and follow Merry into the house. Harcourt shadowed the man. He wasn't taking his eyes of this Sir Seton for one second.

Merry led the way into the drawing room that was almost fully refurbished now. All the paintings were hung, and the furnishings cleaned. It looked like the perfect space for Merry, and Harcourt did not like it one bit. It gave her yet another reason to refuse him.

"T-this is an interesting house." Sir Seton peered around, his hands shaking as he pulled off his gloves and clutched them tightly. Sweat clung to his upper lip. Harcourt narrowed his gaze at him. Something was not right about this man, that much was certain.

"You say you are a relation?" Merry indicated to one of the chairs. "Please sit."

Sir Seton shook his head. "I will stand if you do not mind. I do n-n-not do very well sitting still." He cleared his throat. "I am your late father's cousin."

Merry nodded. "I recognized the name. But why have we never met?"

"We did when you were a little girl, but you would not remember me, and it is unlikely your father would mention me. My wife had family in Scotland, so I-I have had little occasion to be in England."

"Why were you snooping around?" demanded Harcourt. "I did see you, nearly a month ago, did I not?"

Sir Seton swallowed and tugged out a handkerchief to dab at his upper lip. "I was. You must forgive me. I k-know my behavior...well..." He gave a shaky smile. "I am not very at ease with people. I wanted to talk with you, but I am afraid my courage failed me."

"Why did my father never mention you?" asked Merry. "Or any of my other family?"

"We had a falling out many years ago, when you were barely two. But I do not wish to speak ill of the dead. Y-y-you have my sympathies, Lady Merry. I am s-sorry for your loss."

"What did my father do?" she pressed.

Sir Seton smiled gently. "Not much. H-he just made it clear that I was not welcome. Someone of my, um, inability to...be...well...normal..." He sucked in a breath. "Your father thought me an embarrassment to the family. When I met my wife, it was made clear that I should not maintain contact. I am sorry, however, that it meant missing out on you and your brother growing up. My wife and I were never able to have children."

Merry grimaced. "Unfortunately, that does sound too much like my father."

Harcourt shook his head. This was getting ridiculous. "Are you really taken in by this act, Merry?" He closed the gap between him and the old man. "What about the windows? What reason have you for prying them open? Or the door? Or the man on the street who tried to hurt her?"

Sir Seton's eyes widened. "Someone tried to hurt you?"

"A man in town," Merry explained. "I do not know why. I thought perhaps it was...well it seems silly now. It was most likely a robbery gone wrong." She shrugged.

"I-I would never wish you harm, my lady. Your mother took a more sympathetic view of me than your father did, and I would never wish her children harm." He glanced at Harcourt. "I swear, I did not touch any windows or doors."

Merry shook her head in disbelief. "I always said it was the wind."

Harcourt shook his head and thrust a finger at Sir Seton. "No, I don't believe it. Too many things happened. You must have been trying to hurt her."

"Accept it, Harry, you were wrong." Merry put her hands on her hips. "To think you had me tiptoeing around as though someone was trying to harm me."

"I wanted you safe," he said through gritted teeth.

"I appreciate..." She dropped her voice with a glance at Sir Seton. "I appreciate that you were trying to look out for me whilst my brother is gone, but I think you took the duty too seriously."

Sir Seton swung his gaze between them. "Why do I-I not give you a moment?"

"Oh, do not run off, Sir Seton. Please," Merry begged.

"Yes, I think you should leave," snarled Harcourt.

Sir Seton hastened out of the room, nearly knocking into a vase on a side table on his way out. Harcourt steadied the vase and turned his attention to Merry.

"You're foolish to trust him."

Merry's cheeks reddened. "The man is clearly no danger to anyone! He could barely stand, let alone try to run me down with a carriage or set someone on me."

"You really think everything that has happened is a coincidence?"

"You and I both know no one has any reason to harm me. This is a far more logical explanation."

"Logical," he scoffed, mimicking her.

She drew in a breath and eyed him. "I know of the Setons' vaguely. I do not doubt his story, but I will ask my aunt to be sure, of course." She pursed her lips. "You were uncommonly rude to him."

"Do you blame me?"

"Yes! Yes, I do. You have been interfering in my life ever since...ever since Father died. I need some space, Harry. How can I even think when you...when you're always around?" She gestured about the room with her hand.

He stiffened. "I did not realize my presence was so unwanted."

"It's not like that..."

He rubbed a hand over his face. "I was only trying to protect you. I only wanted you safe."

She nodded stiffly. "I know. But there is no danger." Merry thrust a finger toward the door. "I think you should leave. I need space. And time."

"You know, Merry, if you were not so determined to deny yourself happiness, you'd see that's the last thing you want."

"Harry, I am done with you telling me what I want!"

"You are so damned stubborn and mule-headed that you do not even know what you want." He gritted his teeth and pushed a breath through his nostrils. "Fine. I am leaving. Perhaps then you will wake up and realize what I have known all along." He straightened his hat. "We are meant to be together."

He swept out of the room and barged past Sir Seton, his breaths feeling hot in his lungs. Blast that bloody woman. Damn her stubbornness. He was done being patient. He was done trying to wake her up to what was happening between them. He could probably pursue her for years and she still would not give in, all because of some pact.

He was done.

Chapter Twenty-Three

"Merry?"

Merry glanced up at all the shoes and skirts that gathered in the dusty dining room. She lifted her gaze upward to find that the shoes belonged to the Spinsters Club. She gave them a weak smile.

"Whatever are you doing on the floor?" demanded Bella. "You shall get a cold."

"I was just..." Merry sighed, looking around at the clutter about her. The house was silent with the exception of the shuffling feet of her friends. She lifted her wrist. "I hurt my wrist."

Lord, she hated how feeble she sounded. She'd been moving furniture alone once more when she'd lifted one particularly heavy sideboard. If her friends had turned up a moment earlier, they'd have seen her practically blubbering from the pain.

Of course, it was not just the pain bothering her. She frowned to herself and tried to remove the image of Harry's hurt expression from her mind.

She'd not meant to be so dismissive or to push him away. But how could she even breathe or think with him around dictating her movements? How could she ensure she remained true to the Spinster's Club? Her Father's cousin had nothing but good intentions and Harry could not see that. She just had to make him go away. She had to.

"Where is everyone?" Arabella asked, kneeling beside her and lifting her wrist to inspect it.

"I sort of...sent them all away," Merry replied meekly.

"But why? I thought you were making good progress." Bella helped Arabella lift her and maneuver her onto a covered dining chair.

"I do not need anyone's help." Merry stared at the floor, unable to meet her friends' concerned gazes.

She could not explain why, but she could not bear to have everyone working on the house after he had stormed off. In truth, she could not bear to get this wretched project finished. It had been a fool's errand. Why did she think she could create a home for herself in such a brief time, all alone?

Arabella slipped a ribbon from her hair and lifted Merry's wrist. "It does not look too bad. Just a little swollen." She began binding the ribbon around her wrist. "A little support will help."

Sophia folded her arms and eyed the mess about the room. Plates that Merry had intended to display on the sideboard were scattered about everywhere, sheets were half on and half off the chairs, and several candelabras waited patiently to be arranged on one end of the dining table.

"Bella, help me with this mess," Sophia instructed.

"Oh, you really do not—" Merry tried to protest but Bella and Sophia started gathering up the plates and stacking them neatly while Arabella prevented her from standing with a gentle hand to her shoulder.

"Merry, you do know there is nothing wrong with asking for help, do you not?" Arabella seated herself next to her. "You need not do everything alone."

"I wasn't..." The words were cut off by a tightness in her throat.

Sweet Mary, she did not understand what was wrong with her these days. She'd never felt so confused and uncertain in her life. Tears burned behind her eyes. She watched her friends clear away the plates and peered at Arabella's delicate handiwork on her wrist.

"Merry?" Arabella gaped at her. "Are you crying?"

Merry sniffed. "No." She drew out a handkerchief from her sleeve regardless, her heart jolting at the sight of the embroidered initials on it. She could tell herself that she did not know why she had been carrying it around ever since Harry had given it to her, but she'd be lying to herself.

The fact was, she had chased him away. She'd done nothing but repaid his kindness and attention with scorn. And now....well, now she regretted it bitterly. It made her chest ache when she considered she had pushed him away so far that he had not been back in days.

She dabbed a tear and Bella and Sophia paused to stand in front of her.

"Merry, you never cry!" declared Bella.

The declaration only made it worse. A sob bubbled out of Merry and she pressed the back of a hand to her mouth. Arabella wrapped a soothing arm around her shoulders. Tears fell rapidly, plopping down onto her dark skirt. Merry sniffed and dabbed her nose, drawing in a ragged breath in an attempt to stop them.

"What is it?" asked Sophia softly. "Does your wrist hurt very badly?"

"Do not be silly, Sophia," Bella snapped. "She would not cry like that from a sprained wrist."

Merry swallowed and swiped a hand across her face. Her eyes felt red and raw and her throat tight still. Bella plopped herself down on the floor in front of Merry and Sophia followed suit. She swung her gaze between her friends' expectant faces. After everything they'd done together, she supposed she owed them an explanation. The problem was, she hardly knew herself. It was so hard to form coherent thoughts these days. Ever since Harry had kissed her really...

"I..." She inhaled. "I suppose that this house...my determination to have it finished was to distract me."

Sophia frowned. "Distract you?"

"From your father?" Bella said tentatively.

Merry nodded. "With being so busy with the house, I did not have to spare him a thought. I think...perhaps I have always been determined to do things alone to prove to myself that I never needed him. But it hurts, you know?" She stared at the handkerchief in her hand, tracing the letters with one finger. "I always wanted his love, even if I did not need it. I suppose a daughter always does."

Arabella squeezed her hand. "Of course you wanted his love."

"I just cannot help think...If he could not love me," she said quietly, "how can I expect anyone to?"

Silence hung about the room. Merry's heart pounded heavy in her chest as her own words echoed through her mind. Was that what it was? Was that really why she had pushed Harry away?

Arabella cleared her throat. "Is there perhaps someone in particular you wanted to love you?"

Biting down on her bottom lip, Merry looked between her friends. How could she admit to them how she felt about Harry? How could she betray them? But she could not lie to them.

"I have been getting quite close to Harry," she admitted softly. Her friends fell silent again. Merry grimaced. "I am sorry. I did not mean to—"

Arabella patted the back of her hand. "It is just, we are not surprised. You have been spending a lot of time together and he seems to care about you a lot."

"I understand if you are angry with me." Merry hung her head.

Bella laughed. "Why should we be angry with you?"

Merry snapped her head up. "The vows! We took vows. We promised we would never marry."

Bella shrugged. "Harcourt Easton is a good man and desperately in love with you. Anyone can see that."

Sophia lifted a brow. "I didn't realize he was *in love* with her."

Bella made a dismissive noise. "Well you never were the most observant of people."

Sophia opened her mouth then closed it. She looked to Arabella. "Did you realize he loved her?"

Arabella lifted a shoulder. "I knew he was fond of her." She peered at Merry. "Does he love you?"

Merry exhaled slowly. "I think so. Well, he said he does. It's so hard to tell with Harry."

"If he has told you, why is it hard to tell?" Bella asked.

Merry paused. He had been upfront from the beginning. It had only been because of his history that she had doubted him. "I suppose I did not want to believe that he might truly love me." She gestured to herself. "After all, I am a spinster in the making and he is the handsome Earl of Langley. Why should he want me?"

"For the same reason, we want to be friends with you, I am sure." Arabella pushed a strand of hair from Merry's face. "You have many excellent qualities. It was only a matter of time until a man saw that."

"I am sorry for not sticking to our vows." Merry twined her fingers together.

"Oh." Bella grinned. "Did you kiss him? You did, did you not? Oh, Miss Merry, you really are the most scandalous."

Sophia coughed. "Bella, you are really not helping right now." She leaned in. "If you really love him, you know we would not stand in your way. The point of the Spinster Club was to protect each other from hurt, but it seems as though you are hurting now."

Sophia's sympathetic tone threatened to set Merry crying again. She had to draw in a breath and hold it before she could respond. "I think it is too late anyway. I have chased him away to Town. I am certain he shall forget me soon enough." She pressed fingers to her forehead. "Who could blame him? All I did was push him away when he was simply trying to help."

"Surely it is not too late?" Arabella asked.

"I think it is." Merry lifted her chin. "Oh well, I guess I shall be a firm member of the Spinster's Club after all."

Chapter Twenty-Four

Harcourt's mother squeezed his arm and motioned to the crowds of people gathered in the garden of Lulworth Castle. Sunlight cracked through the clouds, warming the lawns where people conversed, ate, drank and played croquet. Aside from the clouds, he knew his mother would consider this garden party a success, with plenty of what she called 'excellent people' in attendance.

"You are being unusually unsociable, Harry," she scolded gently.

"I am here, I am drinking, I am eating, I am conversing," he told her.

"That is not socializing!"

"If that is not socializing, I do not know what is."

She scowled at him. "You have been out of sorts ever since you vanished off to London with Lord Thornford for a week. Not even the return of Daniel has perked you up."

The return of Merry's brother had been the only reason he had returned. Or perhaps it was not. Fool that he was, he needed to see Merry again. Running away with his tail between his legs was not his style, and he hated himself for fleeing in a sulk like a damned child. But Merry had him at a loss. She loved him—he knew it. He'd seen it when she'd told him about the Spinster's

Club. That had not changed, but how long could one flog one-self in the name of love?

He grimaced to himself. A lifetime, he imagined. Merry had been eating into his soul for years and now there was no way of ridding himself of her. The only cure for this was to persuade her to marry him, once and for all. He just was not sure if he even had the willpower to go through another battle with her.

"I am perfectly well, Mother," he assured her, leaning in to give her a kiss. "A man needs a break from the country every now and then."

She tutted. "We are hardly living in the most rustic of areas. Anyone would think we live in some heathen, barren land, the way you speak of escape."

"Do not forget you like to spend most of your time in Bath, Mother."

His mother rolled her eyes. "That is entirely different. I am allowed to wish to escape for a while. I spent many years dedicating my time to your Father's estates and the local people."

"Forgive me, Mother. I am suitably chastened." He gave a wry smile. "I know you deserve to do whatever you wish."

"I have no wish to chasten you, Harry. I am just concerned that is all. Many a woman would be thrilled her son is no longer playing the rogue but the lurking in corners and avoiding people is certainly not like you."

"All is well I promise, and do not fear, I have little intention of playing the rogue any longer. I think I am a little past that now."

She chuckled and shook her head. "So long as you do not become too tiresome, my dear. A woman likes a little rogue in her man." She eyed the crowds of people in the gardens. "Everyone is missing Lord Thornford. I had so hoped to find him a match before he went back to London."

"He shall return I am sure. He has a new love for the country, I believe." In fact, Harcourt fully suspected he would be back sooner rather than later. Griff still could not get over the fact that Miss Bella Lockhart has refused him and had spent the entire journey to Town, plotting as to how he would get his revenge.

"Oh, there is that Sir Seton fellow." His mother lifted a glass in the direction of the wiry man who was doing an even better job of avoiding conversation than Harcourt was. "He's a little odd. Stammers a lot."

Harcourt nodded. "He is not at ease with people it seems."

"Merry says he is quite nice once you get to know him, but his ways take some getting used to."

Gritting his teeth, Harcourt nodded. Since the arrival of Merry's relation, all had gone back to normal. Merry had not been besieged by carts or men with knives or anyone threatening her life. Harcourt had been able to dismiss the private investigator after he had dug into Seton's past. The man was who he said he was, and while he was a little strange, he was utterly harmless. Harcourt's desire to protect Merry had all been for naught. If he were a different sort of man, he'd be utterly humiliated, but he did not think he need to apologize for wanting her safe. Merry likely still thought differently though.

Drawing in a breath, Harcourt snatched up a glass of punch from the table behind him. "I shall go and try to make him welcome. After all, he is a relation of Merry's and we should be welcoming."

"A fine idea." His mother beamed with approval. "Rather you than me. I seem to utterly terrify him," she added.

"You terrify everyone," Harcourt teased, darting away before his mother could scold him.

He approached Seton who was also nursing a glass of punch and gripping an uneaten slice of cake. The line of sweat that seemed to perpetually sit on his upper lip glistened in the sunlight. Seton jumped when he noticed Harcourt.

"Ah, Lord Langley. H-how pleasant to see you. Quite a party." His Adam's apple bobbed.

"I am glad to see you again, Sir Seton. The last time I saw you, I am afraid you caught me in rather a bad mood."

Seton gave a shaky smile. "Merry did explain that you were t-trying to help. I cannot be unhappy that a man like you was looking out for her while she was all a-a-alone."

"You will forgive my rather brutish behavior?"

"Of course."

Harcourt scanned the gardens. Merry's friends were in attendance, along with many others but he had yet to see Merry. "Is Merry here, do you know?"

"Well, her brother is, but I have yet to see her. Perhaps she is at the-the house," Seton suggested. "With her brother's help, it looks to be ready very soon." He smiled. "I can see the appeal in wanting to be alone."

Damn it. Somehow, he felt that once Merry was in that house, it would be even harder to persuade her to leave her impending spinsterhood.

"Do you plan to stay in Dorset long?" Harcourt asked, continuing his study of the crowds.

"D-dorset is certainly different to Scotland b-but I would like to continue getting to know my relations. They have been quite welcoming, and Daniel and his wife are quite wonderful." He nodded toward Harcourt's mother. "Your mother is an excellent hostess. How lucky you are to have such a woman in your life to aide you, my lord."

"She is something, that is to be certain." Harcourt smiled to himself. "Why do you not come and tell her so yourself? I am sure she shall be pleased to hear as much."

"Oh I do not—"

Harcourt ignored his protests and motioned for his mother to come over. She scowled but he knew she would not wish to appear rude. Seton's cheeks blazed almost bright red.

"Sir Seton has been saying what a fine hostess you are." Harcourt grinned at his mother's discomfort. There, let him make up for all the times she had thrust him at strange women.

"I should go and speak with Daniel." Harcourt motioned to the gardens. "Why do you not give Sir Seton a tour of the gardens, Mother?"

"Oh well, I—" She bit down on her lip and clasped her hands together, but not before shooting him a glare. "Of course. Sir Seton, will you follow me?"

Harcourt watched them stroll into the gardens and tried to suppress the smile twitching his lips. He meant his mother no ill will but perhaps she would now understand how it felt to be thrust at people he had no inclination to spend time with.

He eyed the crowds, his gaze falling on Merry's friends. Still no sign of Merry. He frowned while he tracked Arabella's movements. She put a hand to her head and moved away from everyone, toward the shaded area of the veranda. Her movements were shaky, and it did not take a fool to realize she was feeling unwell.

Striding over, he took her arm as she moved unsteadily toward one of the benches.

"Oh." Her eyes widened.

"Let me help you."

She inhaled audibly, the sound shaky. "Thank you." The words were hardly a whisper.

"You're feeling faint?" He eased her down onto the bench. She nodded.

"Should I get you a cold drink?" Harcourt suggested. "Or one of the ladies to tend to you?"

Arabella shook her head. Though normally pale, against the yellow of her silk gown and her fair hair, she looked especially ashen. "I do not wish to make a fuss. Please, do not ignore your guests on my account." She waved a hand toward the people scattered about the gardens.

Harcourt studied her and shook his head. "I think I would rather remain here." He sank down onto the bench beside her.

"I am fine, really."

He shook his head. "You nearly fainted, Arabella. Merry would have my head if I let you swoon and harm yourself."

Arabella smiled softly at the mention of their mutual friend. "I'm not so sure about that."

He wanted to ask what she meant by that but could not quite find it in himself to quiz a poorly woman. "Is it the heat?" he asked, though the day was hardly the warmest of the summer, but with all these stays ladies wore, who knew when one of them might go fainting on one?

"No. It's...well, it was silly."

"Nearly fainting is not silly."

She glanced at him. "Many men would say fainting is very silly."

"Faux fainting is silly indeed, especially when it is intended to garner the attention of a man. That was no fake swoon, however."

Pressing her lips together, she fingered the ribbon trailing down her skirt. "I thought I saw someone. From my past. He should be returning soon, and I am horribly aware of that." She gave a little trill of a laugh. "The poor man has no idea how he might affect me either. He is just here to tend to his mother."

"He has not harmed you? Because if he has..."

She shook her head quickly. "No. It was not him. it was his brother. But I am fearful of his return. It will bring it all back you see."

"I see."

"I am sure this all sounds foolish indeed."

"Not at all. If a man mistreated you—"

"He ruined me." The words came out quickly, on a whisper. Harcourt managed to keep his expression neutral as her eyes widened. "Forgive me, I should not have said such a thing."

"I hope you do not think I am an indiscrete man, Arabella."

She peered up at him. "I have shocked you?"

He laughed. "Not at all. Being in the center of London society exposed me to enough gossip to last a lifetime. I am not so easily shocked."

"He promised me marriage you see. And I thought for so long that he would come back and marry me. But I was a fool."

Harcourt curled a fist. "He was a cad."

"Yes. I know that now." She gave a faint smile. "Please, you must not neglect your guests any longer on my behalf."

"I would not leave you in such a state."

"I just need a moment," she insisted.

Harcourt stood. "Very well, but if you need anything..."

"Thank you, my lord. I can see why you and Merry are such firm friends."

He did not mention that he was not even sure if they were that, especially when his gaze caught on something. Or someone. Finally rid of the black and gray that did nothing for her, Merry moved through the crowds, a delicate splash of lilac that had his gut clenching at the sight of her. He watched her approach her brother. His heart ached.

He understood it now, why Merry had been so wary of him. He might not have ever abandoned a woman after taking her innocence, but the gossip columns did not care much about how honorable he was and paid far more attention to the quantity of ladies he had bedded. He likely did not seem much better than the rogue who had taken Arabella's innocence and clearly left her still shaken. He still could not quite get past the annoyance that she had misjudged him so, however.

He turned on his heel and headed into the house. A cowardly act indeed, but if he was to face her, he needed a little something more than punch to steal him. Especially when she looked so damned beautiful.

Harcourt opted for the library. To the rear of the house, he would not be disturbed there and fool that he was, he wanted to recall the times Merry had become lost here as a little girl—before she was tainted with stories of ruination and heartache. Opening the drinks cabinet, he poured himself some generous fingers of Scotch and settled in the wingback chair by the window. He'd only taken the tiniest of sips before the door opened and he tensed.

"It's not like you to hide in libraries."

He dug his fingers into the arm of the chair. No doubt she had little idea how beautiful she was. The flowing lilac fabric flattered her long figure, cinching in under her bust and drawing his attention to Merry's breasts. Her cheeks were a little rosy and her hair was coiled up with tiny strands touching her neck.

Damn, damn, damn.

He lifted his glass. "It *is* like me to want a stronger drink, however. My mother mixes the punch rather weak."

Merry closed the door gently and moved toward him. Her steps were hesitant, and he noticed a slight tremor in her body. She glanced around, avoiding his gaze when she came to a stop a couple of feet from him. A few moments of silence stretched out before she cleared her throat.

"Arabella told me what you did for her."

He let his brow furrow. "She would not let me do anything. Couldn't even persuade her to have a cold drink."

She tilted her head. "You showed her a kindness."

"I hope you do not think me that much of a rogue that I would not attend to a lady in distress."

"Of course not." She hesitated. "But I do hope you will not mention anything she said. You can imagine how much scandal such information would cause. Not even her family knows, and they would be heartbroken if they found out."

He clutched the drink in his hand and eyed the liquid before throwing it back and savoring the warm burn as it slid down his throat. He placed the glass on a side table and shook his head. "Surely you know me better than that, Merry?"

Merry looked to the floor then lifted her gaze to his, a soft smile gracing her lips. "Yes, I do." Before he could quite fathom what was happening, she was in front of him. She put hands to either side of his face and leaned over. "I do know," she insisted. Her lips grazed his, sending a lightning bolt of sensation through him. He remained frozen. If he moved, he might put an end to all this and he'd be damned if he ruined this moment.

"I know it all," she murmured. "I know what a fool I was to keep denying you. I know that you are not who you were when you were younger. I know that you were right about us."

Chapter Twenty-Five

Merry drew back to look into Harry's eyes. She held her breath. He was annoyed with her, and rightly so. She had doubted him over and over, despite knowing the truth. Harry was not the rogue he once was, and even then, he had always been good and kind to her. And with her friends' blessing, she had no reason to continue denying this to either of them. She kissed him again before drawing back.

"Do you know that I love you?" he asked, his voice hoarse.

Relief nearly overwhelmed her. She laughed and pressed her forehead to his shoulder. "Yes, yes I do." Lifting her head, she grinned. "And I love you, Harry. So much it hurts. I do not even know how that happened."

His lips finally curved into a grin and he smoothed his hands up and down her back. "I do. You bewitched me."

She tilted her lips. "I do not think anyone in their right mind would accuse me of being capable of bewitching men."

"Perhaps I am not in my right mind."

"That sounds more plausible."

He pressed his hands under her bottom and eased her onto his lap. His hands came up to cup her face. "I will not take no for an answer again, Merry. You will marry me."

She briefly debated teasing him for such an abrupt proposal but did not have it in her. Thank the lord, he had not sent her away. Thank the lord, he still loved her. She gave him a swift kiss instead of replying.

"Is that a yes?"

Nodding, she uttered breathlessly, "Yes."

A grin cracked across his face. "You will not regret it, Merry." He pressed his fingers up and around her face to draw her down to him. "I promise you will not regret it."

"I know," she murmured against his lips, allowing herself to become lost in the warm taste of him. She knew it all. As soon as she had heard he'd returned, she'd known...

She had to try to apologize, she had to hope he still felt the same about her, that he was not too angry at her that he would not forgive her. She'd known she could not live with herself if she passed up the opportunity of a life with Harry. Spinsterhood, it seemed, was not for her after all.

He groaned when she flattened her palms against his chest and pressed the kiss deeper. Her skin felt itchy, her clothes too hot. The scent of books mingled with his cologne, creating a heady fragrance that almost had her giddy. He kept hold of her face as though he never wanted to let her go while he kissed her over and over, taking everything she could possibly give. She rocked against him, causing another groan to rumble up in his throat. The sound sent skitters through her and made her stomach twist with excitement.

She broke the kiss and saw the uncertainty in his eyes as she slid off him. She backed away a few steps then smiled, turning her back to him.

"Help me with the laces, Harry."

The muffled sounds of voices in the garden and the sound of her faltering breaths filled the air. She could not bring herself to turn around and face him. Merry pressed her hands to her ribs, willing her breaths to slow. Had she gone too far? Had he changed his mind? Lord, would he not touch her already?

A creak of a floorboard had her heart threatening to burst from her chest. She swallowed hard and dropped her hands to her side. Warm fingers brushed her hair from the back of her neck and she shuddered.

"I will not ask you if you are certain, Merry. I know you never do anything of which you are not certain. But I will remind you that if I do this, you will be mine—forever."

She smiled to herself. "A sacrifice I am more than willing to make."

He chuckled and pressed his lips to her neck. Shivers skimmed down her spine. She moved her head into his touch. His fingers worked on her laces and she could feel a little uncertainty in his movements. Air fluttered over her shoulders.

"Stop," she said softly, when he had unbound her dress down to the base of her back.

He halted, and she twisted to view him. His jaw ticked, he stared at the ties in his hands. Merry reached up and grazed a hand across his jaw, drawing his gaze to hers. Her dress slid from her shoulder and his gaze dropped to the revealed skin there.

His hand shot out and it hovered above her shoulder, his hand shook.

"Have you changed your mind?"

He snapped his gaze up to hers and she noticed a hint of vulnerability dancing in his expression. "God, no," he rasped. His hand closed the gap in a sudden rush of movement, pulling a gasp from her while he groaned. "I was just thinking that once I touched you, there would be no going back, and I would be taking you like the rogue that you think I am."

"Thought you were," she corrected. "But perhaps I do not mind a little bit of roguish behavior."

Shifting her shoulder slightly, her gown slipped further down one side, suspended just over her breast. Her breaths came rapidly as she moved closer to him, causing his hand to drop. He dipped a thumb underneath her gown and rubbed over her hardened nipple.

Merry sighed and closed her eyes as he caressed over her aching breast. When he made no effort to go any further, she opened her eyes to find him staring at her.

With a slight shrug of her shoulder, her gown slipped completely off her breast and his hand covered the unsteady beat of her heart through her stays. Ever so slowly, he moved to cup it through her undergarments and excitement quivered inside her. Merry lifted her chin and met his gaze.

"You need not be gentle with me."

Harry cursed and buried his fingers in her hair, pulling her to him for a kiss. His lips skimmed across hers, nibbling and sucking as if she were some rare delicacy and her legs quivered at the intensity of it. Her nipples chafed against his waistcoat and she moaned at the exquisite sensation. He absorbed her moan, probing his tongue into her mouth and she met it with relish.

Skimming her hands down between them, she worked on the buttons of his waistcoat. He shrugged off his jacket with haste. It dropped to the floor with a thud and he drew back to allow her access to his shirt.

Carefully, she loosened each button, all the while never leaving his darkened gaze. As she leant forward, he brushed a kiss across her forehead, sweeping his thumb over her cheek. She helped him yank his shirt over his head and she smiled at the rumpled image he made with his hair in disarray. Creases appeared around his eyes but Merry could not smile.

She stared at him as he straightened, his muscular chest flexing with every breath. It seemed daunting now, and though she longed to reach out and run her fingers down that broadness, she found herself hesitating.

A glance to his face bolstered her resolve. She wanted this man. Wanted him more than she had ever wanted that house, or to finish her translation. Harry was everything she needed—her other half she supposed. Without him, she really would have buried herself away and become an ageing spinster with only books for friends. He reminded her she wanted more from life.

She wanted him.

Extending her hand out, tracing it down the ridges of his stomach, she watched his muscles contract under her touch and she could hear the harsh rasp of his breath, but he remained motionless, allowing her exploration of him. Her other hand joined in now, skimming over his collar bone until she flattened both palms over his chest.

His throat worked as she traced her finger down it before placing a kiss at the base of his neck, where his pulse flickered erratically. Bringing his hands up to clutch her head to him, he let her nuzzle into his smooth skin, inhaling the musky scent of him. He dipped his head to nip at her ear, his hot breath sending shivers coursing through her.

His fingers worked at her stays then pushed the garment, along with her dress, to the floor. He stepped back to admire, then bundled her to him. The shock of the heat of his chest against hers had her head swimming. He skewed his mouth across hers, and his fingers pressed into her back.

She whimpered at the friction and he hissed as she shifted her hips to meet his, pushing against his rigid manhood. He dragged his hands away and made quick work of the rest of his garments. Her breath caught, and she could not help stare at him. Sweet Mary, all those Greek Gods had nothing on Harry.

Tentatively, she reached out and carefully explored the length of him. She curled her hand around him. "Did I do this to you?"

"Yes." he grated out.

Ever so slowly she released him, drawing her gaze back to his. "Touch me. Make me yours."

"Yes," he agreed, taking her into his arms.

She buried her face into his neck as he carried her over to the fur rug in front of the empty fireplace.

As he laid her down gently, she could not tear her gaze from his body. No wonder she had struggled so much to fight this need for him. The heady desire blurred with the warm sensation of love in her chest.

He positioned himself next to her, propping himself up on his elbow and his gaze traced her length. She tried to keep the heat from flowing into her cheeks under his study, but likely failed. No man had ever seen her like this and the desire to cover herself made her fingers twitch. But if she was going to prove she loved him, that she trusted him, she needed to bare herself to him—in so many ways.

Plucking out a few pins and spreading her hair about her, he fingered the waves as they fell over her breasts and hips. She rose to meet his touch, her lids flickering shut of their own accord, lips parted in a quiet moan. Silently, he traced his finger down her profile, pausing to dip into her mouth. Her tongue instinctively darted out to meet his fingertip and a slightly strangled sound came from him. His fingers continued down the arch of her neck before dipping between her breasts and circling around each nipple.

"Harry," she whimpered.

He answered her with a searing kiss as he clasped his hand around her breast, his fingers scraping over her hardened nipple. Merry met his kiss eagerly but he pulled back.

Ignoring her sounds of protest, he moved back, and she soon became absorbed in the kisses that he lay upon her sheening skin. She writhed underneath him, gasping at each touch of his lips upon her flesh. Harry kissed down her collar bone, lavishing attention on her breasts before moving down, brushing over her quivering belly. His fingers finally tracked a path to the juncture of her thighs and he admired her before stroking across the sweet damp heat that awaited him.

She jolted at the touch, but he placed a large, reassuring hand on her stomach, holding her down before tentatively touching his tongue to her folds.

She jerked as a bolt of sensation rumbled through her, setting her skin alight. "Harry!"

Quickly overcoming her shock, she marveled at the teasingly blissful feeling of his mouth upon her sex and she answered his every move with a thrust of her hips as she curled her hands around his head. A rumble of pleasure at her response erupted from him, causing her enjoyment to increase until she was thrashing, grabbing wildly at the rug beneath. When she felt she could take no more, he slid a finger into her slick heat and she exploded, crying out in surprise and wonder.

A luxurious lethargy cascaded over her and she looked at him with heavy lidded satisfaction. He slowly crawled his way back up to her, his muscular body covering hers. He was careful not to place his weight upon her but she enjoyed the feel of Harry's hard thigh settling between her legs and his solid chest pressed against her sensitive skin. Merry brushed her hands over his rolling muscles, using her fingers to sketch a path over each individual muscle as he framed her head with his hands

She drew in a breath. Was this really about to happen? They locked gazes. His dark eyes were filled with an indefinable intensity, but she knew without question that it was the same love and desire that was likely written in her own expression. His mouth stayed in a grim line despite the obvious pleasure he took from having her beneath him.

Her forefinger tracked the line of his mouth and she smiled. "Why so serious?

His throat worked. "I do not wish to hurt you."

Merry knew she should be nervous—she had heard enough gossip to understand that the first time could be painful—but she could not deny herself this. She wanted more from life than books and solitude. She wanted Harry, and all the scandal that came along with him, including making love to him in the library. Hands to his rear, she coaxed him forward.

In response, he settled between her legs, burrowing his head into her hair and kissing her neck. Cautiously he edged toward her as he nipped and sucked at her ear. Little could distract her from the hard heat of him as he brushed against her and finally found entrance. With a hurried thrust, he pushed into her, filling her completely. She cried out at the sudden pain, tears forming as she clenched her eyes shut to block out the discomfort.

He waited then, apologizing again and again in whispers, brushing the tears from her cheeks. As the sting dissolved, she became aware of a budding heat, deep in the pit of her stomach, and the awareness spread as she finally registered the joy of their union. He must have been aware of the change as he pulled his head from the crook of her neck to meet her gaze. Tears glittered in his eyes and he pressed a fierce kiss to her lips.

Cautiously he pushed forward, and Merry intuitively responded to the slight movement with the raising of her hips. He inhaled sharply as the movement brought him in deeper than she thought possible. She mourned the loss of the pressure in her when he pulled back, but was immediately gratified once more when he lunged again, causing a delightful friction.

Harry picked up the pace, rocking into her and pushing against her body so that it created a tingling sensation throughout her. His breathing grew ragged and soft cries left her. The lamplight danced across the planes of his hard body, enticing her more.

She leaned in and kissed him, tasting all that pent-up desire they were finally sharing. His gaze locked with hers as his hips slammed into her. Clinging to his shoulders, she moved with him, seeking some end she did not completely understand but knew if he was taking her there, it had to be extraordinary. Tingles raced through her, pushing her, dragging her, forcing her over the edge.

Her breath caught, she tensed. The tendons in his neck tightened and she dug her nails into his flesh. Never breaking eye contact, she gave into the tension, letting it wash over her in delicious waves.

Harry's whole body tensed. "Christ, I love you, Merry." The words came out raw.

"I love...you too," she managed to reply.

He closed his eyes and his body shuddered. He groaned, low and deep. Merry felt the pulsing deep inside her then his body relaxed. After several moments of her smoothing her hands along his back, he lifted his head and kissed her forehead.

"Did I not tell you, Merry?"

She gathered her breath. "Tell me what?"

He smoothed back her hair. "How perfect we would be together."

"So smug."

"I certainly am. Look at the beautiful woman I have in my arms." He kissed her lips. "You can admit it, you know?"

"Admit what?" She smoothed her hands along his arms, her body still flush with warmth and a luxurious lethargy.

"That I was right."

Merry shook her head. "You shall never let me forget it either, will you?"

"Is that you admitting I was right?"

"Perhaps," she said with a smile. "But I might need a little more proof."

He chuckled. "As you will, my lady. As you will."

Epilogue

"My goodness, Merry, the house looks wonderful." Arabella gazed about the second drawing room.

Merry smiled, leading Arabella, Sophia, and Bella into the room and motioning for them to sit. "I cannot take all the credit I am afraid. I had a lot of help once Daniel returned."

Bella flung herself down on the chaise longue by the window, spreading herself out as though she owned the place. She grinned. "Now that you are set to marry Easton, are you going to use this as your little hideaway? An escape from the pressures of the life of a countess perhaps?" She waggled her brows. "Or perhaps a nice little private place for the both of you?"

Merry could feel heat flow into her cheeks. Such was the effect of the thought of time alone with Harry. It was still another month until their wedding, and she had to admit to growing impatient. She shook her head, leaning over to pour tea. "Isabel's mother is going to move in. She is a little frail and it would not hurt to have her near."

"That's kind of you to offer her the house," Arabella said.

Merry lifted her shoulders. "Well, it is not really mine to offer, though Daniel did give me the option of keeping it. But I will have no need for it after the wedding. It seemed silly to keep it to myself."

Sophia dropped sugar into her cup and gave it a vigorous stir. "And so he should have offered. You put in most of the work."

"As did you three," Merry reminded her.

Bella pressed her lips together. "I think we made things worse, did we not?"

"Well," Merry glanced at one of the pictures they had hung that was still slightly askew, "not completely worse."

Sophia chuckled. "I think we had fun doing it." She paused. "I think. My toes have still not forgiven Bella."

"I did not even drop it hard." Bella made a dismissive noise. She leaned back. "Is it true Easton thought you were in danger, Merry?"

Merry gave a little nod.

"Why did you not tell us?" Sophia demanded.

"Because it all sounded preposterous!" She grimaced. "And it was. All coincidence. The house was steadily falling apart with the recent winds we had and I heard tale that there was robbery by knifepoint in Brycesbury the very same day Sophia and I were there. It was just rotten luck."

"Well, we were not actually robbed," Sophia pointed out. "Harcourt rescued us if you recall."

Lifting the plate of biscuits from the table, Merry offered them about. "We were lucky there. Or at least, lucky he was so determined to protect me from a non-existent threat."

Sighing, Bella pressed the back of a hand to her head dramatically. "If only I had been there. What I would not give to be rescued by a man."

Sophia gave Bella a jab in the ribs with an elbow.

"What?" Bella straightened. "One is allowed to dream occasionally, is one not? It does not mean I *really* want a man."

"Nor do any of us," Sophia reminded them. "We might be one member down, but the Spinster Club still remains."

"Oh yes." Bella nodded. "I have no intention of marrying, even if our founding member has abandoned us."

Merry opened her mouth to protest but quickly closed it when Bella shot her a teasing look.

"Good, nor do I," said Sophia firmly. "Lord Easton is one of the few good men around, and now that Merry has snapped him up, I see no need for any of us to marry."

"I do not mind admiring, though." Bella folded her arms across her chest. "You cannot deny me the odd flirtation, surely?"

Sophia shook her head, lifting her gaze to the skies. "You will scandalize us all, Bella."

Bella shrugged. "Well, if we are not to marry, what does it matter if we are scandalized?"

"You could be sent away to Ireland like poor Miss Lucy Gable," Arabella reminded her.

Taking a long, noisy sip of tea, Bella made a dismissive noise. "Father would not notice if I flung myself at the Prince Regent, I suspect."

Sophia nodded. "Thank goodness I live alone."

"You are certainly not missing out on anything. As soon as I can decide how to gain my independence, I am leaving them all for good." Bella pursed her lips. "Perhaps I could become a courtesan."

Arabella straightened. "Most certainly not!"

Bella grinned. "I was jesting. Though sometimes anything seems better than remaining at home with my awful brothers." She gave a mock shudder. "This morning they woke me up because there were no sausages for the morning meal. Apparently, it is up to me to ensure we are always well-stocked with sausages." She shook her head. "It is not like there was not enough food!"

Merry leaned over and gave Bella's hand a squeeze. Though Bella jested more than most, she knew her brothers were a handful. If not worse. They were spiteful men who looked down upon their sister.

"We shall figure out a way of gaining your independence, but you know we shall all support you in the meantime. You could always come and live with me at Lulworth Castle."

Shaking her head vigorously, Bella made a horrified expression. "Just as you did not want to be intruding on your brother's new marriage, I have no wish to become your companion, Merry. You and Easton are far too in love."

Sophia lifted a brow. "Is there such a thing as far too in love?"

Bella nodded. "There is when one is the only company for the couple. I shall simply have to find some other solution to my situation."

"You are always welcome to come live with me, Bella, you know that," said Sophia.

"We would probably kill each other if we lived together." Bella slumped back on the chaise. "Face it, I am stuck there until I think of something immeasurably clever. Unfortunately, I have very few skills."

"You're a wonderful harp player," pointed out Arabella.

Bella waved a hand. "Anyone can play the harp."

Merry laughed. "I certainly cannot. And even if I tried, I would not sound anything like you."

"I thought we came here to talk of Merry's impending marriage, not my harp-playing."

"Will you not miss the solitude?" asked Arabella. "I know how much you like to be alone to do your work."

"Harry has promised me plenty of space to finish my translations, so long as I emerge sometimes and pay attention to him." Merry suppressed a smile. She suspected that would not be hard. She'd seen him only yesterday and she missed him already.

Bella eyed her in awe. "I never thought you would be the first to fall, Merry."

"I have no intention of falling." Sophia lifted her chin. "I enjoy widowhood far too much."

"And I certainly never want to set eyes on a man again," added Arabella.

"Men are the worst," Bella agreed. "With the exception of Easton," she added quickly.

Merry smiled sheepishly. "I am sorry that I did not stick to my vow."

"Never mind, you can be an honorary member." Bella patted the back of her hand. She lifted her cup of tea. "To the Spinsters Club."

"The Spinsters Club," the rest of them echoed.

"Long may we rule over men!" Bella added with a wink. "None of them stand a chance."

THE END

About the Author

USA Today bestselling author Samantha Holt lives in a small village in England with her twin girls and a dachshund called Duke. She has been a full-time author since 2012, having gone through several careers including nurse and secretary.

Read more at www.samanthaholtromance.com.

Printed in Great Britain
by Amazon